Dear Jeanette

I hope ... getting ... Grenadine

HEADLIGHTS, DIPSTICKS,
& MY EX'S BROTHER

♡ your coolest step-sis

HEATHER NOVAK

Heather

EDIE'S AUTOMOTIVE GUIDE: VOLUME 1

HEADLIGHTS, DIPSTICKS, AND MY EX'S BROTHER

By: Heather Novak

This book is dedicated to my girlfriends, for your stories.
To Janna, because you pulled this book from the depths of my weird brain.
In loving memory of Dash, who was the best doggo ever.
And to Sergeant Cornflakes—I hope wherever you are, you are still crowing at 3:00am.

To every woman who has ever felt like Edie—this one's for you.

"BELIEVE IN YOURSELF and you will never go wrong." – Mom
Letter to Heather, 7/22/1990

CHAPTER ONE

EDIE'S TIP #42: BLINKER FLUID IS NOT A REAL
THING, REGARDLESS OF WHAT THOSE AUTO SHOP
GUYS TELL YOU.

THERE WAS ONLY one ballroom in Grenadine, Michigan and it wasn't big enough for the both of us. I had no choice but to take a third—or was it a fourth?—champagne glass to keep my fist from finding its home square in my ex-fiancé's throat. The fizzy bubbles tickled my tongue as I silently congratulated myself on my self-restraint. His perfectly tailored gray suit was new, but the purple striped tie had been a birthday gift from me two years ago. Asshole.

His dark brown eyes snapped to mine before quickly blinking away. He wouldn't come over; confrontation wasn't his way. He would just spend the evening passive-aggressively glancing at me and then telling my family he hoped I'd found "some stability" after our "devastating breakup." The comment would spiral, as small-town gossip always does, and make everyone believe I'd gone off the deep end. And business would continue to plummet.

New life motto: never ever, ever (again) get romantically involved with someone you share a business with.

An arm slipped around my shoulders and I looked up from my seat to find the bride, my younger cousin, Kristy, smirking at me.

"Edie, what's with your 'I'm going to punch someone' look? Make sure to use your elbow so you don't break your thumb. Again."

"Yeah, yeah, love you too."

She kissed the top of my head and I smiled, leaning against her awesome cleavage. "Your boobs look phenomenal," I said, garnering a raised eyebrow from a nearby table.

"Don't they?" her new husband Sam said reverently. "Thanks for picking this dress." The ivory dress complemented the pink undertone of her light skin, and it fit like a glove. He was right; she did look absolutely smashing. He smiled at her, love and adoration filling his eyes. I bit my lip, looking away from their intimate expressions. I was so happy they'd found each other.

I gestured between the two of them. "Congratulations, by the way! Sam, you should've run while you had the chance. You're a hostage now."

He kissed Kristy's hand, the movement making her beautiful ring sparkle under the thousands of twinkle lights. She thumbed the gold band adorning his dark brown skin, her lips curving into a smile. "Hostage, huh?" he asked. "Good thing I have great company." Kristy rolled her eyes but smiled so large my cheeks hurt for her.

I leaned over. "How many 'Oh! I didn't know he was black' comments have you gotten so far from the extended family?" I whispered loud enough to get a few more side-eyes from the neighboring table.

Kristy and Sam looked pointedly at each other, then back at me. She tilted her head to the side. "Now, are we counting the rehearsal dinner when Great-Grandma Mildred told him he was a terrible waiter?"

Sam rolled his eyes. "Or that weird second cousin of yours who thought I was LeBron James?"

I winced. "Dude. You really shouldn't play anything sportsball related."

He pointed at me. "Accurate."

Kristy was the athletic one—basketball, soccer, golf, she could do

2

it all. Sam, however, couldn't catch a ball to save his life. But he looked damn good in a pair of glasses, holding a book.

My mother's laugh cut through the ballroom and a chill ran down my spine, successfully chasing away the warm, fuzzy fog of alcohol. That was my mother's patented I'm-about-to-make-a-scene laugh. I threw back the rest of my champagne, preparing for the apocalypse. "By the pricking of my thumbs, something wicked this way comes," I muttered, grabbing Kristy's drink from her hand and finishing it too. It had far too much rum—any rum was too much rum, let's be honest—but I soldiered through. I was a trooper like that.

"Holy crap," Kristy whispered, leaning over my shoulder. "Is that? No way..."

"Is that my mother with her hand on Will's chest?" I narrowed my eyes, the seven layers of mascara protesting the movement. "Why, yes. Yes, it is."

The man I'd thought I'd spend the rest of my life with was leaning just a little *too* close to my mother and smiling as she whispered something in his ear. My stomach tightened in the same way it had when I'd found that three-week-old banana in my duffel bag after a road trip. To be fair, it could also have been all that alcohol combined with a lack of food...

"Why? How?" Kristy whisper-shouted. "He definitely wasn't invited! Is she trying to hook you guys back up?"

"I mean, her older sister's daughter is getting married at twenty-four, a whole year younger than *her* daughter. I wouldn't put *anything* past her." I shrugged, trying to be nonchalant. By Kristy's well-practiced side-eye, I could tell she wasn't fooled for a second. "What? Don't look at me like that. I want nothing to do with him. I thought throwing all his stuff out the window was a pretty clear message."

She frowned, then turned to study Sam, who had suddenly become very interested in his cufflink. "Samuel, what do you know?"

He sighed, resignation pulling his shoulders forward. He clasped her hands in his and kissed the top of each one. "My dearest wife, please forgive me."

She raised an eyebrow. "You're so weird. What am I forgiving you for?"

He flashed her a sheepish grin. "Your mom told me Aunt Cynthia demanded a plus one. You were stressed out, so we didn't tell you and just added an extra chair to the family table."

She cocked her head and studied him before nodding. "Good man. I would've committed homicide if I had to do that seating chart one more time, and then I wouldn't have gotten to wear this pretty dress." They kissed, eliciting some hoots and a chorus of silverware clanging against long-abused glasses. Kristy smiled but growled low. "Remember to use plastic glasses when you get married," she advised me before kissing her husband again.

My mother's laugh rang out again. Jami, my older brother, weaved through the crowd in his impeccable navy blue tux. He jumped onto the small platform that housed the head table. "Mayday, mayday," he said. "We better start the speeches before Mom laughs again. Twice is a warning. Three times is detonation."

As best man and self-appointed disaster-avoidance coordinator—a full-time job, really—Jami's advice was heeded immediately. Kristy and Sam signaled their DJ to begin the speeches as I stood to snag another glass of champagne from a passing waiter. My brother snatched it out of my hand and put it back on the tray. "Nuh-uh. Your cheeks and ears are turning pink and you have the maid of honor speech to give. How drunk are you?"

I snatched it back. "Whatever. I'm as pale as a ghost. I turn pink with a four-degree temperature change."

He grabbed it back from me and drank it down. I pouted.

Then my mother laughed for the third time. Into a microphone.

We both froze.

"Ground control to Major Tom," I whispered, spinning to face the woman—nay, *dragon*—who had somehow given birth to both of us. All of the delicious alcohol in my bloodstream disappeared and I was suddenly stone cold sober.

Mom's ice-blonde curly hair was perfectly straightened and coiffed, magically hiding the devil horns beneath her impressive mane. Her floor-length ivory ball gown—because really, what else would she wear to her niece's wedding?—glittered as she lifted the microphone to her mouth with one hand and grabbed Will's hand with the other.

"Oh, this can't be good," Jami said.

"The last time she had a microphone, she told my senior class about getting knocked up with me!" My face heated from the memory. Grenadine High School Class of 2010's prom had gone from fairytale-themed to an abstinence lecture the moment my mother found the microphone.

Jami shook me, breaking me out of my trance. "I'm going to go stop her before this turns into her telling the entire summer camp at the closing ceremony that you started your period."

I let out an exaggerated sobbing sound. "Oh my God, I forgot about that." Guiding me by the shoulders, he pushed me down into my chair and then speed-walked toward my mother. I slumped, defeated. Why was I always the one she made look bad in these microphone exchanges?

I glanced around, trying to see where our plan for speeches had failed. Kristy and Sam hovered on the edge of the dance floor with a shocked Aunt Mary blustering about the order of speakers. Really, Aunt Mary should've known better than to leave any audio-visual equipment unattended. My mother could sniff out a microphone hidden on Ford Field during a blizzard in mid-February.

"Now, I know it's Kristy and Sam's day," my mother said, and I pressed my palm to my mouth to keep from laughing out loud. No, she most certainly did *not* know that. "But I believe they would be as happy for me as I am for them!"

"Timber!" I whispered, making a falling sound, followed by an explosion. Kristy's other two bridesmaids, both cosmetology school friends who clearly hadn't known what they were getting into with this wedding, looked at me with identical expressions of horror. I slid lower in my chair, hoping to slip under the tablecloth and stay there until tomorrow morning.

"This afternoon, William asked me to marry him and I said yes! Third time's a charm, ladies. So from one happy couple to another, congratulations, Kristy and Sam!"

The sound of screeching brakes filled my ears and the room tilted sideways.

No.

Nope.

God, I was drunker than I thought.

I needed an ambulance. I was obviously dying. At least hallucinating.

I couldn't have heard that right.

But then why was my mother—MY MOTHER—locking lips with my ex-fiancé in the front of a ballroom? Lips that until eight months ago had belonged to me? Oh God, he was dipping her backward like a scene in a movie. He'd never kissed me like that.

I was losing my mind.

This didn't mean what I thought it meant.

Like, she wasn't *engaged* engaged, right?

Glancing around the room, I spotted the table of my mother's best friends—the pack she'd brainwashed into adoring her—swooning. Why had Kristy even invited them? Stupid small-town inclusiveness. One of the Barbie bombshells was dabbing at her eyes with a monogrammed handkerchief. Another was clapping above her head as if she were in church and the pastor had just said something enlightening.

My gaze snapped to Jami, who was wrestling the microphone from the dragon's claws. "Congratulations to my mother and William and cheers to Kristy and Sam," he said quickly before turning off the device and handing it back to the DJ. My mother raised her right hand and gave her queen wave, making sure to blow a few kisses to the audience.

I needed to move. I needed to get out of here. I couldn't feel my legs.

Kristy let out a sob, then slapped her hand over her mouth, turning away from me. Sam had his arms around her, probably trying in vain to convince her that the reception wasn't ruined. I wanted to tell her not to cry because it would destroy her amazing makeup. But if I'd been in her shoes, I'd probably cry too.

Oh God, I'm not crying, am I?

Somehow, I unclenched my fists and pressed my palms to my scalding cheeks. No wetness. Good. I wasn't crying. I could *not* show weakness in front of these hyenas. I could already hear the gossip from the nearby tables.

"Did she know?"

"Obviously not, look at her face."

"Poor thing. I can't even imagine losing a guy like William to *my mom.*"

"There must be something really wrong with Edith if he prefers Cynthia over her."

The DJ, clearly struggling for what to do next, mumbled something about the rest of the speeches happening soon before playing an upbeat swing track. I wrapped my arms around my middle, trying to convince myself I didn't want to throw up.

I closed my eyes and concentrated on tuning out everything around me. *Deep breath in, deep breath out.* When I was 90 percent sure I could stand without fainting, I opened my eyes and searched each corner of the room, looking for a quiet and easy exit. I didn't want to make Kristy's wedding even more of a spectacle, but I couldn't stay here another moment. I knew she'd understand.

The closest door to me was the kitchen, which probably had a back door. I plastered a giant smile on my face and stood, gripping my clutch as if it were a life preserver. *Good. You didn't fall flat on your face. Now, put one foot in front of the other. Smile, SMILE!*

I had to make it past three tables and fifteen feet of open floor before I walked through the swinging double doors. I could do this. Each step was carefully calibrated to be fast, but not look like a run, and not cause me to fall on my ass. I hated heels.

I waved and smiled to those calling my name, even uttering an "I'll be right back!" and "So good to see you!" in a clear and calm voice. *Move aside, Frances McDormand. The Oscar goes to me.*

I slipped into the kitchen and inhaled a deep breath of relief, leaning against a nearby wall. I tucked my hand just below my collarbone and concentrated on slowing my heart rate before I passed out. All this wedding needed was an ambulance. Especially an ambulance after my ex had announced his engagement.

José, my employee Rosa's older brother, walked by with a tray of full champagne flutes. Without saying a word, he handed me one and gestured to the kitchen's back door. I made a mental note to give Rosa a raise. I lifted my glass to him in a silent toast and all but sprinted into the humid July evening.

New life motto: never ever, ever (again) go to another wedding.

CHAPTER TWO

EDIE'S TIP #12: VINYL IS FOR YOUR HIPSTER RECORD
COLLECTION. NOT FOR CARS. OR PANTS.

IT WAS A STICKY EVENING, which did nothing to dampen the burning ball of rage inside me. Maybe I was part dragon after all. My phone kept pinging with texts, but I ignored it as I stomped down the main road.

Memories of my mother's reactions to my canceled engagement took on new meaning. Cries of "William's too good of a man to let go" and "Someone is going to snap him up immediately and you'll regret this" made much more sense now. I was triple glad I'd thrown all of his shit out the window. Bastard.

An ill-placed step off the side of the road broke the heel off one of my towering shoes and I almost dropped my champagne glass. That would've been tragic. Deciding not to risk it, I finished the rest of the delicious alcohol and then kicked off my nude pumps.

I stuck my tongue out at them in disgust.

Like an adult.

Grabbing them with one hand, I glared at the offending shoes. My mom had bought them for me because she said my flats would be an "embarrassment." I chucked the shoes and glass into the roadside ditch. A string of expletives that would've made my mother clutch her double strand of real pearls burst from my mouth.

I stumbled forward, but quickly righted myself and brushed back the hair clinging to my face. Despite the thousands of bobby pins and several layers of hair spray, not even a professional team could keep my blonde hair at bay, much to my mother's dismay. It was fine but thick, rejecting hair clips and going wild in humidity. It had a mind of its own.

I sang a few verses of my favorite breakup anthem while I walked along the grass on the side of the road, adding in a few twirls and fist pumps. But as I neared my shop, a *cock-a-doodle-doo* from my pet rooster, followed by a car door slamming closed and a man swearing, stopped me in my tracks. For the first time, I realized walking alone at dusk while everyone I knew was back at the venue might not have been my best choice. Of course the last "crime" this town had seen was the high school football team tipping Mr. Benson's cows after the homecoming game.

I took several giant steps to the side of my building and peered around the corner into the parking lot. "Hello?" I called, my voice shaky. "Sergeant Cornflakes?"

To his credit, Sergeant Cornflakes, my guard rooster, waddled forward, squawking. Though he was probably just angry I hadn't fed him in several hours as opposed to warning me against an intruder.

"Sergeant Cornflakes? Really?" asked a man whose voice made my heart stutter. I hadn't heard it in so long, I was almost afraid to hope. He walked around the front of his sensible 2010 Ford Explorer, which was haphazardly parked in my auto shop's parking lot, and leaned against the hood. My rooster darted back over to him and pecked at his feet. He looked down at the bird. "This is somehow your fault. I know it is."

Unable to contain the bubble of elation that rose inside of me, I ran toward him, nylons be damned, and launched myself into his arms. *Him*, my brain said. *It's him!*

"Luke!" I cried, and he chuckled.

"Reeses!" he whispered, using a nickname I hadn't heard in years. My obsession with the peanut butter and chocolate snack was legendary. This wonderful man used to sit on my front porch and share a package of candy with me when I had a bad day.

He pulled me tight with one arm around my waist, lifting me off the ground and swaying back and forth. "Oh my God, what are you doing here? Besides scaring my rooster." Sergeant Cornflakes was making a racket at all of our commotion. I shushed him, and he flapped his wings at me before waddling away.

Luke lowered me to the ground and rested his chin on my head for a long moment before releasing me. "What are you doing walking down the road with no shoes on? And why do you have a rooster?"

I shrugged. "The rooster found me. Just showed up a few months ago like he owned the place." I stepped back, searching his face. "What's going on?"

"I'm in town for a few weeks and decided to blow a tire in a pothole. Stopped by the shop since it's actually really hard to change your tire when you don't have a spare. Just been hanging out since you closed early..." He gave me a once-over. "For a wedding?"

I nodded. "Kristy's wedding. And I've already complained four times about the pothole on Freemont and Porter, but it appears the city just wants me to keep selling tires." I raised an eyebrow. "No spare?"

"Long story." Luke ran a hand through his dark hair. "Kristy and Sam finally tied the knot? He's a brave man."

I would have laughed if I weren't so startled by how the years had changed him. His Rallye Green eyes—I'd color matched them to a Camaro color chart when we were kids—were grayer, made darker by the shadows under them. The crease in his brow was deeper and I resisted the urge to smooth it out with my thumb. A dusting of hair on his angular jaw was flecked with gray.

The natural swagger he'd had when simply *standing*, the same swagger that had gotten him out of detention more often than not, was gone. This was the same lost boy who'd stood in front of his mom's grave ten years ago. His shoulders hunched forward, and he took a deep breath, as if trying to keep himself upright.

Thirty was too young to look this fatigued, this exhausted with life. I put my hand on his arm, unsure of how to find the carefree, larger-than-life friend I used to look up to. The man who used to take me four wheeling and cliff diving when I was young enough to feel invincible. Now he looked like he wanted to crawl into bed for days, maybe weeks, and hide from the world.

Standing in the dark, touching him after so many years apart, especially when he looked so *human*, flipped something inside of me. A low buzz started in my chest, as though I was standing next to a live wire. My eyes snapped to his and he lifted his hand, brushing my escaping hair back behind my ear. I took a deep breath, trying to slow my suddenly racing heart. *Calm down, heart! It's only Luke.*

"So when's your wedding?"

I flinched and stepped back. "Um." I laughed uneasily. "When was the last time you talked to Will?"

"To be honest, it's been a while. I texted him about some business a few weeks back and that I was coming for a visit. That's about it."

I sucked in my lips and looked at my shop, nodding. "You have a key. Why didn't you go in and make it easier on yourself?"

He shrugged. "Just because I have a key doesn't mean I'm welcome."

I grabbed his forearm. "You're always welcome." I squeezed once and then let go. "Come on." I fished my keys out of my clutch, opened the front door, and then flipped on the interior lights. I raised the bay garage door under the large Pop's Auto Shop sign, that had a banner hanging underneath that read Edie's Auto Shop. While Will had agreed to the name change as an engagement present—one of the few good things he did before we ended—I couldn't afford to update the sign yet. "Get inside. I'll grab Cornflakes and make sure he's not going to wake the neighbors."

"Why is he even awake right now?"

"He's an insomniac."

"Only you would have an insomniac rooster."

I pursed my lips, then nodded. "That's probably true." My dumbass bird stood pecking at a spot in the middle of the road. I sighed. This was my life. "Sergeant, you get over here right now!" He lifted his head, crowed at me, and then went back to eating what looked like rocks. I stomped after him, leaned over, and scooped him up.

The screech of tires and the blare of a horn turned my limbs to ice. Something hit me hard and shoved me to the ground, out of the way of the speeding car. It had no headlights on, but the lean frame of a FIAT 124 Spider and red skunk stripes were a dead giveaway.

My heart tried to crawl out of my chest while my rooster tried to claw off my arms. I let him go. "Fried chicken would be really good right now," I warned. A shaken Luke pulled me off the ground and against his chest. He was breathing hard, his hand firm on my back. "I'm fine," I said. "I'm okay. Thank you."

He didn't let go. I resisted the unexpected urge to lean closer to his really, really nice chest. So warm and hard...*Edie. Stop it.*

"Hey, you okay?" I asked, pushing back slightly. "Did you hurt yourself?"

Seemingly remembering himself, he cleared his throat and stepped back. "I'm sorry." He looked after the car that was now long gone. "I didn't get a good look at the license plate."

I shrugged. "I know who it was. Rebuilt that transmission last week. I'll call it in to Sheriff Jasmine."

We looked both ways before crossing the street. "Is she at the wedding?"

"That's why I'm going to do it immediately, so she can escape." I held the door open and Luke brushed past me. Whatever magical combination of cologne, soap, and deodorant that made him smell like *him* washed over me. It made me feel as though I had finally come home after too long away.

I shook my head to clear it. Maybe I was still drunk. *Must actually drink water soon.*

After calling dispatch and reporting the near hit-and-run and throwing some serious shade at my rooster, who was now curled up in a tire inside the shop, I shoved my feet into an extra pair of sneakers I kept in the main office. I wobbled a little as I stood up from my chair, the alcohol and exhaustion from a week of wedding madness catching up with me.

Luke ran up and grabbed my arm. "You're not okay."

I waved him off. "I'm fine, just a little tipsy and a lot exhausted." I rubbed my forehead. "Let's get this tire changed."

He laughed and shook his head. "You're going to fall over. Let me walk you home and I'll change it. Just tell me how much I owe you for the tire."

"I can fix a car drunk, blindfolded, and with one arm tied behind my back," I countered.

He lifted his hands in surrender. "I know you can. But tonight you don't have to."

"Well then, let me introduce you to someone." I motioned with my head to the bay at the end of the garage, where I had built a protective wall around my baby. Entering the code into my keypad, I unlocked the side door leading to my treasure. "Come into my real office. Lucas Moretti, this is Ella-Jean. Ella-Jean, meet Lucas Moretti."

He stopped dead in the doorway, his eyes going so wide I thought they'd pop out of his head. "Holy shit," he breathed reverently. "A 1967 Camaro Rally—"

"Sport Coupe," I finished for him. "Grandpa left it for me in his will. It was hidden in a storage unit that not even my nosy mother knew about. I've been restoring it when I have time."

"That is amazing. Manual transmission?"

"Obviously."

"Ram-air intake?"

I just looked at him with an eyebrow raised. "And, before you ask, I ordered the dual exhaust chrome tips two days ago."

"Hardtop?" he asked, then looked at me. "I would've thought you'd be a wind-in-your-hair woman."

"Hardtop. Vinyl is for records, not cars."

"I think I'm in love."

"Yeah, me too."

"Obviously, you're in love with Will."

"I was talking about the car. I love the car. My mother says I'm incapable of loving a person, and it's why I'll be alone forever."

He opened his mouth to respond, but nothing came out. "What does that even mean?" he finally managed.

I walked around Ella-Jean and opened the driver's door, climbing in. The seat's off-white leather was worn and desperate to be replaced, but she still felt like a glove against my curves. Luke stumbled into the car, plopping down hard. He stared at me, even while running his hand over the dash. "What happened?"

I lifted my left hand and showed him the bare ring finger. "Eight months ago, I realized I didn't want to marry Will."

He frowned. "Eight months?" he rasped, his eyes narrowing. "Why...why didn't you tell me?"

I let my hand fall to my lap and folded my fingers tightly, shrugging. "I just assumed he did. I know you guys don't talk much, but I figured you knew."

He shook his head. "I would've..." He let out a breath and turned to look at the windshield. "I dunno. I would've done something."

"I'm sorry. That was poorly done of me. I just thought it'd circulate, you know?"

He reached over and squeezed my knee. "It's okay, Reeses. Grief is messed up."

I nodded.

"What happened?"

I unclasped my hands and started to pick at the loose stitching on the steering wheel. "It was always just assumed Will and I would end up together, even when we were dating other people. Our families viewed other relationships as placeholders. Hell, maybe I did too. We were only a few years apart, both stayed in Grenadine, were childhood friends. Then after Grandpa passed and we inherited the shop, Will was around a lot."

I stared down at my nails, which were already starting to chip. I hadn't opted for the fancy gel polish because it'd just come off the moment I started working on an engine. I had spent hours soaking and scrubbing to get my hands clean for today. Even with gloves, my skin was always dirty from the long hours at the shop, something Will had hated.

I rested my right arm over the top of the wheel, staring out the windshield as if I were driving. "I loved him, until one day, I didn't. It's like, as we grew up, we grew apart. I started not to like who I was with him. Then out of the blue, he proposed—a huge public scene—and I said yes because I didn't know what else to say. But more and more every day it felt like I was going through the motions to hang onto something we weren't anymore. I wasn't happy or excited or counting down the days."

Luke reached over and grabbed my hand and squeezed. "So you ended it?"

I laughed without humor, moving my hand away and swiping at the sudden wetness in my eyes. "We were in a standoff about where we would live once we were married. I always imagined growing old in my house, ya know? But he wanted to buy a new house, a bigger place with better updates. Maybe I should've considered it, I dunno. Maybe I was so desperate to latch onto something to get me out of whatever tug-of-war our relationship had become..." I shook my head.

Luke looked appropriately horrified. "He didn't take it well."

"He had just started his realtor business, said the market was hot. We fought, he apologized, I thought it was a done deal. Then one day I came home to see a For Sale sign in my lawn. I threw all his shit out the window."

"Wow." He blew out a breath and leaned back in the seat. "How'd your mom react?"

"She took it worse than either of us."

He glanced at me. "Not surprising."

"Nope." I sighed. "I saw the signs she was dating someone new. New jewelry, more requests to watch Clementine, twice a month salon visits."

He blinked at me. "You're not saying what I think you're saying."

Embarrassment warmed my cheeks and I pushed out the words. "I didn't realize she was dating Will."

"Well, fuck." He blew out a long breath and ran a hand down his face. "I can't believe...that's just so..."

"Preach." We sat in silence for a long moment. "My mom just announced their engagement at Kristy's reception. Before cake too, which I think is just rude."

"Wait, WHAT?!" He jerked to face me, jaw swaying in the breeze.

"Breathe."

He moved his mouth, but nothing came out. Clearing his throat, he tried again. "Your mother. And my brother?"

"Yes."

"Cynthia is going to be my...sister-in-law?"

I pursed my lips and nodded.

He shook his head slowly. "I don't even know what to do with this information."

I gestured to myself. "Hence why I'm tipsy. And not at the wedding. I left before cake. *Before cake.* I was cake-blocked."

"Of course you're thinking about cake right now."

I elbowed him. "I helped pick it out. It was triple-layer, chocolate, hazelnut, raspberry, and dark-chocolate-ganache perfection." They'd even made a cupcake for me that was free of my food allergens. Now it'd go uneaten. So sad.

He groaned and for a moment I forgot what we were talking about. That sound made my heart flutter, which was weird. I rubbed my chest for a moment and sat up straighter in my seat, giving us more space.

"Can we sneak back into the ballroom and steal cake?" he asked.

"I would do anything for cake," I said in a sing-song voice. "But...I definitely won't do that."

His laugh was almost as good as his groan. "Oh Edie, I've missed you." He sighed and closed his eyes. "There's something I need to talk to you about." He opened his eyes and watched me for a long moment. My stomach did a somersault.

Whoa. What was happening? I cleared my throat. "Is this 'something' going to make my night worse?" He nodded, confirming my worst suspicions. "Please wait until tomorrow. I'm at max capacity tonight."

His hand found mine again and this time, I didn't pull away. Palm against palm, I felt his heartbeat, all the words of comfort he didn't need to say. That strong, steady pulse warmed me from the inside out and I caught myself looking at Luke just a little closer. He really was incredibly handsome.

"I've been trying to save enough money to buy Will out, but the last few months have been hard," I finally admitted, trying to navigate out of this weird tension building around us. "Why your father and my grandfather thought it would be a good idea to leave this place to all of us, I have no idea." I forced out a what-can-you-do chuckle.

Jami was already in law school and had told Grandpa he didn't want a share of the shop. Kristy was never a car enthusiast, either. How I wished Grandpa had given it to them anyway, if nothing else than to help me with Will's drama. Luke was silent, but he tightened his grip on my hand.

"I should've ended it with Will sooner than I did. And less dramatically. I should've called you right away to talk about the shop. I just...couldn't."

"You don't need to explain it to me."

I leaned my forehead against his shoulder and breathed deep. For the first time in a long time, I was finally getting enough oxygen. "I've missed you," I admitted.

"Missed you too, Reeses. I would've come back sooner if I'd known."

I shrugged. "And done what?"

"Something. Anything."

He released my hand and wrapped his arm around my shoulder. It was everything I needed. It had been so long since a man had held me like this. The butterflies in my stomach started swarming. *This is just a platonic hug,* I told them. *It's Luke.*

But maybe that was the problem.

It was *Luke.*

It was the boy who'd worked with Grandpa and me under the hood while Will worked with his dad in the office. It was the teenager who'd punched Justin Kenzer in the face for making fun of me in fourth grade. It was the guy in his midtwenties who'd called in every favor to get permission to take me to my senior prom while home on leave from the Marines when my high school boyfriend dumped me just two days before. It was the man who took a red-eye to be by my side for a few hours at Grandpa's funeral.

Realization washed over me, and I jerked upright, turning to stare at him, wide-eyed. My breath quickened as I took him in: his mussed, oil-dark hair, his light olive skin, his thick eyelashes, and his soft, bowed lips.

He smirked and raised his eyebrows. "What's that look for?"

Just coming to the realization that I may have a few non-platonic feelings for you. "I—uh...just..." Oh, this was bad. So very, very bad. I could not like Luke.

"Yeah, sounds about right." He leaned forward, and I scooted back against the door so fast my elbow hit the window crank. I hissed and wrapped my hand around my traitorous limb. He laughed and grabbed my knee, pulling me toward him. "Hey, what's going on? You know you can talk to me."

"That's what I'm afraid of," I said before my brain caught up with my mouth. I really needed to fix whatever misfire was going on there. I blamed it on that clean, masculine scent hanging between us. Oh God, I'd forgotten how good a handsome man could smell. It was like a drug. I took a deep breath through my nose, getting high off an evergreen, citrus, campfire combination.

He smiled, and I just stared. I wanted to keep that smile in my pocket and pull it out whenever I was lonely. I wanted to savor a sweet mouthful of it whenever life got too sour.

Whoa, Edie. Calm down. He's just Luke. But it was like a glass barrier had shattered. He was no longer *just* anything. And my fuzzy head wasn't working fast enough at putting the barrier back in place.

"You're having an infamous freak-out right now." He sighed. "I can hear it in your silence. Reeses, come on. Talk to me."

I didn't say a word. Instead, I did just about the stupidest thing I could think of.

I leaned forward and kissed my ex-fiancé's older brother.

CHAPTER THREE

HIS LIPS WERE soft and warm, and the moment they touched mine, my entire body came to life. I was kissing Luke. I WAS KISSING LUKE?! This was not how I'd expected this night to turn out.

My lips moved against his top lip, then his bottom one. The rough scrape of his stubble made my stomach somersault. Choirs sang a hallelujah chorus in my head. My heart did a tap dance. I was drowning in him, his scent, his heat. It was like a movie moment I wanted to replay over and over again.

Until suddenly, a very important realization pushed its way through the chaos and I froze.

Luke *wasn't* kissing me back.

I pulled back, covering my face with my hands. "I'm so sorry. It was just the alcohol—"

"No, no, it's okay," he said, his voice a little shaky. "It's just not a good—"

"Idea, I know. You're going to be my step-uncle after all." I swear I vomited a little in my mouth.

He groaned. "Oh God, never call me that again." He gently

clasped my wrists and pulled my hands away from my face. "Edith, look at me."

I kept my eyes squeezed tight. "Nope, because I just made this super awkward and weird and this night is already really terrible so I'd just rather pretend that none of this ever happened, okay?" I was rambling.

He hesitated, as if he was going to say something else, but then released my hands. He cleared his throat. "Whole thing's forgotten."

Was it just me or did he sound a little...sad? That's it. I was never drinking again.

A knock on Luke's window made me scream, and like the graceful, delicate lady I was, I flailed. My hand hit Luke's nose, my elbow jabbed the steering wheel, my foot whacked the door panel, and my bracelet got tangled in my hair. Because this was the night that just kept on giving.

With Luke's help, which of course required him to lean over me and made my punch-drunk heart flip out *again*, I was freed. I finally scrambled out of the car only to come face-to-face with a very pissed-off Jami.

My brother's glacial glare made me cringe. He was all soft brown curls and brown eyes, but he could go from teddy bear to ice queen in two point five seconds. "I've been calling and texting to make sure you're okay. You just took off and didn't let me know that you got home."

I raised my arms in a "look, I'm all in one piece" motion. "I'm sorry. I'm fine."

"Clearly."

The other car door opened and Luke stepped out, his lips in a tight smile. "Jami, it's good to see you again." He reached out his left hand and Jami shook it quickly.

"Luke." Jami's tone was lined with frost.

"What is your problem, J? I'm fine. Luke blew a tire and came by the shop. I left my cell in the office, I'm sorry."

He pinched the bridge of his nose. "Did you tell her why you're here?" he asked Luke.

"Not your business, James Joseph," I countered. "Leave him alone."

"Save it, Edith Doreen."

We stood there with our arms crossed, fuming. I could practically see the little hand-drawn comic strip swirl above my brother's head.

"Jami's right," Luke said. "I know you wanted me to wait until tomorrow, but I should've insisted. Especially considering the circumstances."

This day was turning out to be really, really shitty. I rubbed my forehead and shook my head. "Just tell me."

He ran his hand down his face and held his palm to his jaw, clearly uncomfortable. "The shop is no longer split between you, me, and Will at thirty-three percent each."

I stared at him, blinking. My chest burned with anxiety, or maybe just heartburn from all the alcohol. Either way, I had a feeling I wasn't going to like where this was going.

"Two years ago, after Dad got sick and the three of us inherited the shop, I bought twenty-seven percent of Will's shares. He still has a few shares left, but I am currently the majority shareholder at sixty percent."

My mouth fell open. "Wait, what?!" I took a step back into Jami, whose hand rested on my shoulder, steadying me.

"Legally, we didn't have to tell you, but he should have. He had invested everything into his real estate business and he needed the money to buy an engagement ring and pay for the wedding. He wanted it to be a surprise. I had the cash, so I agreed. I assumed he'd discussed this with you after the proposal."

I covered my mouth. This was too much for my brain to handle. My ex had definitely never told me any of this. I shook my head to clear it. "Okay, so what else?"

"I'm back because I'm selling all of my shares. I need the cash and it can't wait." With his admission, something dark passed over his expression. His Adam's apple bobbed with a hard swallow before his eyes met mine. The desperation in them probably matched my own.

"Who are you selling to?" I whispered.

"To your mom."

I swayed on my feet, grabbing Jami's shoulder for balance. "You what?"

Luke shoved his hands into his pockets and looked at his feet. "Figured it was best to keep the shop in the family. Will told me he didn't have the liquid cash, but Cynthia did. I didn't know…"

"She'll be the majority holder," I said. It wasn't a question. "Which means my mother will have her dream—control of the shop." And there it was, the one thing that could possibly break me.

Mom *hated* the shop. Some of my oldest memories were of her storming into my grandparents' house and absolutely losing her shit when she saw grease on my hands. Over the years, her temper had grown quieter, although just as cruel, and her hate for the shop had never ebbed. A hate that no one knew outside of the family, not even Luke. My mother was good at showing people what she wanted them to see.

Jami put his arm around my back, supporting me. "Edie, it's not just the shop. It's the land too." Sometimes I hated having an attorney for a brother.

Luke ran a hand over the back of his neck. "I know you and Cynthia don't have the best relationship, but it was her dad's shop and now she'll get to share it with you. Maybe it will help you two grow closer together."

No. It wouldn't. But how would Luke know? He hadn't been back for longer than a few days in years. *"You've always loved the shop more than you love me!"* she had screamed at Grandpa, and then me, time and time again. *"You save all your love for stupid cars!"*

I sagged in defeat. "How long have you known?" I asked, looking up into the face that so closely mirrored my own.

"About a week," Jami admitted. "You were busy with the wedding and I decided to wait to tell you."

Somehow, I managed to nod, as though I understood. "When?"

"I'm here for about three weeks," Luke replied.

I turned to look at my brother. "And he can sell even if I don't agree?"

Jami leaned his head against mine. "Decisions for the shop will be determined by the majority, at sixty percent or above. So yes, he can legally sell the shop. Your choice is whether to sell your shares or stay on with the new owner."

I put my face in my hands. "I think I'm going to be sick." I was going to lose my shop and my home with a few signatures on a piece of paper.

Luke sighed. "Listen, to me, the shop is yours. It's always been yours and it should've always been *only* yours. I just need the money, and it's all I've got left to sell that's worth anything."

"To my mom."

"The agreement with Cynthia is verbal only. I haven't signed the contract. If you can earn the money or if we can find another buyer, I'll sign it over."

"How much?" I looked at him through my fingers.

"One hundred seventy-five thousand. But I'll negotiate down to one fifty, if you can do it."

I laughed, but it came out more like a strangled sob. "And there're no other options?" I looked at my brother.

Jami shook his head.

"I...I..." My head started pounding as if I had a rubber band winding tighter and tighter over my eyes. "And no one told me?"

Jami shook his head. "I wasn't the one who did the transfer."

I could feel Luke's eyes on me, but I couldn't bring myself to look at him. Instead, I looked at my Camaro, wishing I could crawl back inside of her and make this all go away.

"Luke, I'll come back and help you change that tire." Jami grabbed my arm. "Come on, I'll walk you home." I stumbled forward but allowed him to lead me away.

Luke stepped toward me and I flinched. He raised his hands up in surrender. "Reeses, it's good to see you, despite the circumstances. Jami, thanks for your help."

I let my brother tug me out of the shop and up the walkway to my house. It was maybe half an acre at most, but tonight it was like miles. Thick silence stretched between us until we reached my front door. Jami pulled out his keys and we didn't speak, just hugged for a long moment before he kissed the top of my head and gently shoved me inside.

I closed the large hand-carved oak door behind him—a wedding present from Grandpa to my grandma—and leaned against it before locking the deadbolt. Usually, I loved coming home to this house that held so many amazing memories. Tonight, every inch of it mocked me.

My stomach rolled and this time I didn't fight it. I sprinted to the downstairs powder room and emptied my stomach contents over and over again. Alcohol definitely burned coming back up.

I fell asleep with my head on my knees, sitting on the bathroom floor.

"I'M DYYYYING," I lamented as I fell down in the chair in front of my shared desk. The door to the tiny office couldn't keep out the clanging and slamming of oil changes, new brakes, and alignments filling up the bays. Gasoline and oil fumes clung to me, making my head swim. But it was a Saturday and we actually had business, so I couldn't be too mad.

Tamicka, my bookkeeper and office manager, looked at me over her rimless reading glasses, judging. "Well, you aren't going to feel better in here."

I lifted my head just enough to stare at her across the desk, where she was *loudly* typing numbers into a spreadsheet. She was nearly ten years older than me, though her flawless deep brown skin made her look like she was still in her twenties. She was crazy smart, always read a dirty book at lunch, and obsessively loved Christmas all year round. She'd been my first hire after Will had vanished, and was the best life choice I had ever made.

"I nicknamed you T-Money because you somehow always find me the money to stay in business. Don't fail me now. I'll rename you T-Broke." I groaned and lowered my head back on my arms. "Never mind, that was terrible."

She sighed and took off her glasses, folding them carefully and setting them on the desk before picking up her pen topped with a Christmas tree. "We need to start making triple our income pretty much immediately. We're operating in the black, but just barely. We're down fourteen percent from last year alone." She looked up at me. "You should've hired me sooner."

"Truth," I said. "Create a buy three oil changes, get one free package. Must buy by next week. Email our entire database."

She made a note on the legal pad next to her. "Buy new brakes for one car, get half off a second car?"

"I'm not made of money."

"Most people have two cars. Even if they don't need brakes yet, they may jump on it. I'm a genius."

I grunted my agreement. "That's why I pay you the medium bucks. So how many of these will we need to sell to make one hundred fifty thousand?"

The chair creaked as she shifted. "It'll help. But..."

"T-Money, come on. Give me something."

She covered the top of my hand with hers. "The liquid cash isn't there. We just had to replace the parking lot after that shit winter. And the lift in bay two. Not to mention the new fridge in the break room, and the plumbing issue—"

"Okay, okay. I get it."

"What about your inheritance?"

I shrugged, then regretted it. Everything hurt. "I have a few thousand. I used a good chunk when we needed to repair the roof." *And even more to pay my staff when we had leaner months.*

She squeezed my hand. "Save it. You'll need it and it's not really going to make a dent. You need to get to the bank next week. See if you can get a small business loan."

I pushed myself upright and rubbed my hands over my face and over my sloppy ponytail, sighing. "Okay, I'll make an appointment on Monday."

I pressed on the center of my forehead, trying to stop the throbbing. Maybe I should just go back to bed. A knock at the door made my stomach gurgle and I groaned a response. My head mechanic, Chieka, walked in and clucked. "Why are you here?"

"Because I'm clearly insane. What do you need?" She walked behind me and started rubbing my shoulders. I tipped my head back and glared, not fooled by her decoy. "See, you're standing there looking like a nice and well-adjusted person and we both know that is a load of bullshit. That's your revenge smile."

She smiled wider. I knew, just knew, she was reveling in some karmic action. "Tell me someone dropped a piano on my ex's head?!"

She rolled her eyes. "Girl, no. Settle. Rich Grouchen is here claiming his engine is fried because you sold him faulty tires last week."

"Why is this good news?" I whined, rubbing my head again. "Tires can't fry an engine. He's delusional."

She winked at me. "Because we have a paper trail of reminder calls and a waiver from his last visit saying he declined an oil change even though he was well overdue."

"Tell me."

"Twenty-five thousand miles overdue."

My mouth fell open. Pretty sure my eyes almost fell out of their sockets. Maybe that was just the hangover. "You're kidding me."

She laughed, low and evil. "It's just so beautiful." She mimed wiping a tear away.

"Maybe he shouldn't have replaced his oil change reminder with his MAGA sticker," Tamicka muttered.

I laughed, then groaned. "Ow. It hurts. But it's worth it."

"Damn right it is," Chieka said. "Now come on. He wants to talk to the owner."

Tamicka stood up and rounded the desk. "I brought popcorn," she teased. "I'm not missing this!"

Chieka pulled me out of the chair. She was Japanese American, five inches shorter than me, and all muscle. Her dark, thick hair was in a long braid, the end of which she tugged on in excitement. She had a twisted sense of humor and I loved it.

Chieka wrapped her arms around my middle and gave me a quick hug. She was frowning when she stepped back. "First off, I can smell the alcohol on you. Second, your hair." She reached up and tugged a few strands back and forth before giving up. "I can't help you. Just go be a badass." She pulled a hairclip from her pocket and secured her braid in a bun at the nap of her neck, ready for battle.

"Aye, aye, captain." With a deep breath, I followed her out and into the foyer where Rich waited.

Grenadine, Michigan was only an hour northwest of Detroit, but I swear some days it was a different planet. Rich was a Grenadine-born-and-bred local who had the social skills of a robot. Will had always worked with him in the past, but without my ex, Rich was forced to talk to me and Chieka.

We embodied everything he feared: two strong women who knew more about cars than he did. Poor Rich. His nightmares were finally coming true.

"Mr. Grouchen, it's nice to see you again." I extended my hand and was happy to discover I didn't burst into flames at the lie. "Chieka was telling me you're having some engine trouble?"

Not bothering to shake my hand, he looked right over my head. "Where's Will?"

"He's not available right now, but as one of the owners and a licensed mechanic, I can promise you that I'm fully capable of answering any questions you may have."

Rich was a white man who looked to be in his midfifties, had a Bluetooth headset growing out of his ear, and was clearly heavily invested in the sweater-over-a-collared-shirt look. I didn't know what he did for a living, but he really needed to take better care of his Chevy Silverado 3500HD, fully loaded. He stepped into my space, trying to intimidate me. "I want to know what you're going to do to fix my truck. You did something to it the last time I was here."

Chieka took a step toward me, her shoulder almost touching mine. She handed me a manila folder, similar to the ones we kept on all of our high-maintenance clients, and I smiled. We were battle ready.

"Mr. Grouchen. As you can see detailed here"—I opened the folder and pointed at several call logs and release forms with his signature—"you declined to get your oil changed by us, despite being part of our loyalty program. This signature confirms that you documented getting your oil changed outside of our facility—"

"I'm not talking about the oil! I'm talking about my tires!"

I breathed in slowly and then closed the folder and looked over at the employee standing in front of Rich's truck. "Rosa, can you please bring me Mr. Grouchen's oil filter?" As if waiting for her cue, and to be honest she probably had been, my youngest employee approached us with a soggy, black ball of slime in one hand, and an extra pair of nitro gloves and a clean oil filter in the other. Rosa was nineteen but could fix almost any engine with her eyes closed.

She handed me the gloves and I snapped them on before accepting the filter. "Let me break this down for you. This is your oil filter." I ran my finger along the edge of it, chunks of black gunk oozing onto my finger. "This is what's circulating in your engine right now. It's why your truck's running poorly."

I nodded at Rosa, who held up the clean oil filter. "This is what a new one looks like. Even though it's the exact same filter model, it's half the diameter of the one we pulled out of your truck. This is why you actually need to get your oil changed when your truck's display advises you to do so. Changing your tires did nothing to your truck. It's the lack of oil changes that are causing the problem."

I gave the filthy filter back to Rosa. "Now, this is what I'm going to do because you're a repeat customer of ours." And Lord knew we didn't need any more bad online reviews from crazy customers. "We will be happy to replace your filter and change your oil right now. After that, we'll give you the name of a dealer in the area that I think may be able to better help you in the future. If you'd like to just go straight to that dealer for your oil change, we'd be happy to give you directions."

Rich blustered, a lot, before yelling a vague threat about suing me and getting into his truck. I spun on my heel and walked out of the waiting room. Chieka was hot on my heels. She closed my door and clapped. I stilled her hands with mine, the ringing in my ears subsiding. "*Shhh*, Mama has a headache."

"I hate to ask this, but can we really afford to be firing customers right now?"

I sat down and looked up at her. "Nope. But there's nothing I can do to help him. He probably already fucked up his engine and he won't do regular maintenance on it. Not dealing with him anymore."

"I love it when you're feisty."

"Yeah, well, love it while you can. If we don't bring in more business, we're going to be feistily finding new jobs." A knock at the door was like a gong, and I decided I really needed to leave. "Deal with that? I'm going home."

"Nope. This is all you." She opened the door and stepped out, trading places with the dark-haired, green-eyed man I never wanted to see again. That was a lie. My heart did a drum solo the moment I smelled his intoxicating scent.

"Luke," I breathed, like an idiot. He smiled at me and holy hell, my champagne-addled memory hadn't done him justice. Freshly showered but still scruffy, he could be a body double for Justin Baldoni. My body hummed with his proximity, because apparently I was still sixteen years old and had zero control over my emotions.

My eyes strayed to his lips, and the kiss I wanted to forget was most definitely *not* forgotten. *He didn't kiss you back and he's selling your shop. Stop it!*

He cleared his throat and I blinked, looking back up at his eyes. "Figured you needed breakfast."

I cringed, hands flying to my stomach. "I don't think I could even smell food without doing something embarrassing."

"You mean like that time you threw up in a trash can after we rode every coaster at Cedar Point? Or the time you threw up in Jami's lap because you were reading in the back of the car on the way to the sand dunes? Or the—"

I held up my hand. "If you value your life, you won't continue."

He bit his bottom lip and crossed his arms, rocking back on his heels. There was movement behind him and I caught Tamicka and Chieka staring shamelessly through the office window. With a huff, I gestured toward the door. "Fine. Get me out of here."

Luke stepped aside, motioning for me to lead the way. As I stomped out of the office, the two troublemakers pretended to be absolutely fascinated with a calendar on the wall next to the door.

"That calendar was one of Grandpa's decorations," I called. "It's from 1974." It was from the year he and Mario, Luke's dad, opened the shop. Luke coughed behind me, covering a laugh. "And I'm taking the rest of the day off."

CHAPTER FOUR

AS WITH EVERY SMALL TOWN, there was only one good restaurant. Ray's was a diner and ice cream shop styled just like it had been in the 1950s: black-and-white checkered linoleum floor, red and chrome stools, and a wide white counter separating the front of the house from the back. Chuck Berry rocked over the speakers as we walked in.

Ray, the owner, was sitting at the cash register reading a newspaper and chewing on an unlit cigar. Despite coming to America from India in the eighties, he had fallen in love with 1950s pop culture and had never looked back. "Hello, hello, hello!" he sang in his deep baritone voice. "How's my favorite mechanic?" He did a double take and pulled the cigar out of his mouth. "And the prodigal son!"

Luke and Ray shook hands and exchanged hellos while his granddaughter, Celine, popped up next to me and pointed to the booth in the back corner. "You'll be less on display there," she advised.

We scooted into to our seats, not bothering to open the menus.

"How long do you think it'll take the Grenadine Herald to post a picture of us on Facebook?" Luke asked, leaning across the table.

The click of a shutter had us both looking at Gerdie Haninky, sitting backward on her stool at the counter. She was smiling while fiddling with her phone. She was eighty if she was a day, but had the fastest fingers in the city.

The old woman winked at me and I gave her a thumbs-up. "I'd say forty-three seconds. Nothing like the *prodigal son* coming home."

He groaned and looked to the ceiling. "Don't start. I'm not a prodigal anything."

"You know this town thinks of you as their own."

He shoved his hand through his hair and grunted. "They just feel sorry for me. 'Look at poor Luke. Can you believe what his father did?' I hate being back here."

I opened my mouth to say something—what, I didn't know—but Celine approached our table. She was wearing a poodle skirt and a pristinely ironed white blouse. Her stick-straight onyx hair was in a high ponytail and swished with her quick movements. "Luke Moretti, you're a sight for sore eyes." She turned to me, her dark eyes twinkling. "And I heard you had quite the shock last night!"

Gossip spread like wildfire in this town. I cleared my throat. "Celine, we're actually having a business breakfast. Think you can grab us some coffee and two specials?"

She tried to hide her disappointment about the lack of gossip with a shallow smile. "Sure thing. One regular, one Edie-special?"

"Perfect." When she departed, I folded my hands in front of me and stared at my friend. "No work talk until coffee is in my mouth." The walk had helped clear my head, but I didn't want to take a chance.

He nodded and picked up a menu from behind the napkin dispenser. After giving it a quick once-over, he looked back up at me. "This menu hasn't changed in ten years."

I shrugged. "If it ain't broke, yada yada."

"What's an Edie special?"

I pursed my lips, wondering if he was going to make a big deal about it like my last date had. Like Will had. I cringed. *This isn't a date, Edie. This is a business meeting. And he's not his brother.* "Remember my migraines?"

His face scrunched up. "Those were awful."

"You're telling me." I tapped on the table. "Intolerant to gluten. I am now officially part of a fad."

He nodded. "So no gluten, no migraines?"

"I get like one every three months now. And even that may be cross-contamination. But yeah, gone." I pointed to the kitchen. "I came in to order an omelet one day and told them about my gluten issues. Ray had no freaking clue what gluten was, but he's been great."

"And now you have an unofficial menu designed after you."

I smiled. "I'm pretty badass."

"Yeah, ya are," he teased. Celine dropped off our coffees and Luke grabbed one sugar and set it next to my cup.

My stomach tightened. He remembered how I took my coffee. *Focus. Coffee.* I needed this caffeine to chase away all the residual amorous feelings I had for the handsome man in front of me. He was just Luke. My oldest friend.

I tracked his movements as he lifted the cup to his mouth and took a bracing sip. His tongue slipped out of his mouth and caught an errant drop on his bottom lip. My eyes widened, and I struggled to take a controlled breath. Maybe two cups of coffee would do it.

A soft smiled touched his lips. "Tastes just like I remember."

Three cups. I was definitely going to need three cups of coffee. I chugged half of my too-hot cup of coffee and somehow didn't pterodactyl screech. Clearing the smoke from my throat—because my insides were on fire—I set my cup down and put my chin in my hand. "So, what are we going to do about the shop?"

He rubbed his eyes with one hand. "I was up all night trying to figure out what to do."

So was I, but for different reasons. I glared at him as if me kissing him was his fault. "Easy. Don't sell to Cynthia."

He smiled sadly. "I need the money, Edith. But if you can find someone else who could be your partner, that'd be great."

"Why? Why do you need the money so bad?"

He shook his head, looking down at the sugar packet he was playing with. "I'm going to try to help the shop pick up business. Maybe I can sell you some of the shares too."

"We'd need a miracle," I snapped.

He nodded. "How many staff do you have?"

"Five, including me."

He shook his head. "We didn't even have five when Dad and your grandpa ran the shop. How can you afford five now?"

I shrugged. "I pay my bills, put the rest back in the shop."

He pointed his finger at me. "You and I both know that's not how you run a business. It's Saturday and you have no line. Five years ago, there was a line down the drive."

"Five years ago, Grandpa was alive."

He nodded and spun his coffee cup on the table. "Is the house paid off? Grandpa owned it for what...forty years?"

I sighed, running my hands through my hair. "I took out a loan when he got sick to pay for the hospital bills and get at-home care." I took a deep breath to ease the tightness in my throat. "I'm still paying."

"Damn." He looked out the window. "What if you were only open four days a week? Cut all but you and one other employee down to part-time. You'll save on operating costs."

"Then my girls and Henry don't get health insurance."

He looked at me. "They can buy their own. And Henry Blinkner? He's like seventy years old. What's he doing at the shop?"

I reared back. "Uh, he was one of my grandpa's oldest friends and he is the best painter in town. His hands are steadier than mine."

Luke shook his head. "Maybe you should stop doing body and engine work. Pick one or the other. You can't afford—"

I put my hands up and leaned forward, whispering harshly, hoping like hell that Gerdie didn't have her hearing aids in. "Listen. I know that you're trying to help, but you do not get to show up, take one look around, and twelve hours later make demands about my staff."

He crossed his arms and leaned forward on the table. "I'm trying to help you."

"Trying to help *me*? Yeah, okay. Not selling would help me the most."

He ran a hand down his face. "Edith."

"Lucas." Then my nostrils flared, picking up the custom scent of lavender, orange blossom, and sulfur.

We both looked up when she cleared her throat, interrupting our standoff. *Great.* Just what this day needed.

One hundred percent more of my mother.

CHAPTER FIVE

EDIE'S TIP #24: CARRY AN AIR HORN IN YOUR
POCKET TO HONK AT PEOPLE WHO ANNOY YOU,
EVEN WHEN YOU'RE NOT DRIVING.

THE SIGH that came out of my mother's mouth was absolutely
Oscar-worthy. I considered clapping, but Luke kicked my shin under
the table. He was always too good at reading me.

"Edith, you're not answering your phone," Mom said, indignant.
Her perfectly manicured nails were wrapped around her designer
purse strap. Her engagement ring was on full display, all four shiny
carats. Why she felt the need to show it off was beyond me. I was
pretty sure it could be seen in the next county.

I made a show of patting my coverall pockets. I had unzipped the
top and tied it around my waist, a look my mother hated. "Must have
left it at home."

She pursed her perfectly painted lips at me. "What if one of your
staff needed to get ahold of you?" She said the word *staff* like it was a
vulgar word. *Go staff yourself!*

"Uh..." I looked out the window, confirming my shop was,
indeed, still only one block over. I could literally see the top of my
sign. "Pretty sure they could find me in an emergency. The bakery
ran out of gluten free flour two days ago. Not a lot of options."

Celine walked toward us with our food and I caught her eye and shook my head. If she dropped off the food now, my mother would either join us or expect us to hear her out before we ate. Neither of those options was acceptable. Thankfully, Celine had been waitressing since she could carry a tray and knew how to read the room. She immediately spun on her heel and hustled back to the kitchen. She was one smart, gluten-free cookie.

"Mom, we're just wrapping up. What do you want?" I asked.

She looked at Luke for a long moment. "Luke, it's nice to see you again. My lawyer is waiting for your paperwork."

He put on his best innocent face. "Oh my word, you didn't get that yet?"

She paused as if deciding whether or not to believe him. "No. Please have it re-sent."

He nodded. "Right away, ma'am."

Celine came back and dropped two to-go boxes and the bill on the table, running away as fast as she could. Luke grabbed a twenty from his wallet and tossed it down before standing up. "Well, Cynthia, it's a pleasure as always. We'll be in touch. Edie, come on. I'll walk you home."

When I stood, my mom turned toward him. "You know, Luke, congratulations are in order. I'm going to be your new sister-in-law." She took a step toward him, getting a little too close. He took a step back into the wall.

I saw red. "Mother! You already snagged one brother. Leave this one alone."

The diner went silent. *Oh shit.* I had said that out loud, hadn't I? I rubbed my forehead as the dull ache returned with a vengeance. This is why I didn't like to *people.* I should've just stayed at home in my jammiest of jammies, curled up on the couch, and complained to Jami about how much I'd had to drink.

Luke's eyes met mine and went wide as Mom turned slowly to face me. I knew I was in trouble. She was a venomous snake who was rattling her tail and ready to bite.

"Well, Edith Doreen, if you weren't so busy living a man's life, maybe you wouldn't have so much trouble holding on to one. Men want pretty things. Not someone with grease under her ragged fingernails." She squared her shoulders. "I try and I try with you. But you just keep on failing me."

Yep, I should've expected that. If anyone else had said it, I would've gone on my feminist-smash-the-patriarchy-women-deserve-pockets-too rant. But she knew where all my insecurities were and directed her spotlight with pinpoint accuracy.

I hated myself for looking at my fingernails. Sure enough, one of my nails had broken sometime between the wedding and the showdown. *Come on floor, swallow me up.* When I looked back up, Luke's eyes were locked on me, dark with anger.

He grabbed our food and put his arm around my shoulder. Everyone who was blatantly staring at our table quickly picked up menus or loudly commented about the weather.

"Smooth," I said loudly. "Almost believed it."

Luke propelled us forward. "Let's go, Edie."

My mother grabbed Luke's arm and he dropped his arm from my shoulder before turning around and carefully disengaging her claw. "We made a deal, Luke," she spat.

He stepped away from her. "We made a deal under false pretenses. Like, I thought you were a decent human being." He pulled me back tight against him as if he was trying to shield me from her wrath. He rushed us outside and down the sidewalk, weaving around a plethora of baby carriages and families out enjoying the summer day.

"Forgive my phrasing, but when did your mother go fucking nuts?" Luke asked.

I laughed without humor. "She usually hides the dragon better. Must be tired from her performance last night."

His arm tightened. "I thought you had an okay relationship? I knew it was rocky sometimes, but not like this."

I shrugged. "Everything got worse after Grandpa died." I knew grief did crazy things to people, which apparently also included turning into a terrible, self-absorbed woman with no regard for her daughter's dreams.

By the loud stomping of her heels, I knew Mom was closing in. There was really no use in running; she could win the Boston Marathon in those shoes. But if we made it to the shop, at least we would be on my turf.

She gained on us and stepped in front of Luke as we reached my parking lot. She crossed her arms and pursed her lips. "You know good and well no one else is going to give you the price you need in cash. My investor will go to two fifty."

Luke tensed and heat burned up my neck. Two hundred and fifty thousand dollars? I couldn't compete with that. Especially not that quickly.

She turned her laser-blue eyes to me, and Luke's arm still around my shoulders was the only thing that kept me from shrinking back. "We're meeting Monday morning at eleven at Missy's to try on bridesmaid dresses. Don't be late."

A single, loud guffaw fell out of my mouth. I shook my head and rubbed my eyes. I was still drunk. That was the only explanation. "I'm sorry, what did you say?"

My mother rolled her eyes, clearly put out at having to repeat herself. "We are meeting at Missy's to try on dresses at eleven." She spoke slowly and enunciated each word. "I already ordered my dress —it's custom so I had to get that started *ages* ago. But you and the girls still need dresses and we don't have much time. And you know with your teenage-boy body, they're going to need to do a lot of alterations."

I was in so much shock, the teenage-boy-body comment didn't even faze me. "You expect me to be a bridesmaid in your wedding to my ex-fiancé?"

She looked bewildered. "Well, of course! You're my only daughter."

I stared at her. "You have two daughters."

"You know what I mean." She waved me off. "Clementine lives with her dad; it's not the same."

"Jesus," I whispered, then looked up at Luke. "I've changed my mind. Let's sell the shop. We'll jump in your truck and just drive until we fall into the ocean."

Mom put her hands on her hips. "I don't appreciate your attitude, young lady!"

I put my hands on my hips. Like mother, like daughter. "Mom! First, I have a meeting with the bank on Monday because, unlike you, I'm trying to save my shop. Second, I am not going to be in your wedding. I am not *going* to your wedding. I'm not sending you a card, a present, or even a text. I will not be at Missy's on Monday."

She looked like I had slapped her. "I don't see what your problem is! I'm your mother! This is your responsibility as my daughter."

Luke stepped between us. "Cynthia, maybe you two could talk about this when you're both calmer." He stared her down and she took a step back under the force of his gaze. My heart skipped a beat. He was standing up for me. No one but Jami had ever stood up for me. Will used to say I was just being mean to Mom and needed to give her a chance. Talk about a red flag.

My mom looked between Luke and me, calculating. "You know, you're going to be her step-uncle soon. A relationship between the two of you would be wholly inappropriate."

"For fuck's sake, Mom! You are marrying my ex-fiancé. Why on Earth would I be in your wedding?"

"Language, Edith. And it's not my fault you let him get away."

Luke *ahemed* loudly. "Cynthia, congratulations on your engagement. Welcome to the family and all that. Edie's had a long night and will call you later."

"No, I won't!" I sniped.

Luke gave me a sideways look. *Not helping*, it said.

"Luke, you have no right to interrupt a discussion between me and my daughter," my mom said in a voice so cold, it gave me chills.

"What would your mother say? Or should I say, your adoptive mother?"

Bull's-eye. This woman was vicious.

Luke reeled back as if he had been shot, and I saw red. Yes, it was true, his dad had an affair early in their marriage, but Caterina Moretti loved Luke as if he were her own. If you asked her, she'd say she would always be Luke's mom, no matter that some other woman had given birth to him and left him on the Moretti's front porch.

I took a step forward ready to get in my mother's face when I heard feathers rustling. I watched in pure joy as my rooster, who'd clearly had enough of the yelling, walked out from the bush behind Mom and promptly pooped on her shoe.

I covered my mouth, trying to contain the laughter that bubbled up inside. He was so getting an extra treat for dinner. When my mother started screaming, I couldn't keep silent. Tears pooled in my eyes as my entire body shook with amusement.

I couldn't even understand her threats as she stomped off to her Audi parked in front of the shop. Instead, I grabbed Luke's arm and bent over at the waist, trying to get a lungful of air. "Oh God, did you see her face?!" I wheezed.

Luke wiped his eyes with the back of his hand. "I'll never forget it as long as I live."

Sergeant Cornflakes waddled by and I scooped him up, petting him. "You're such a good birdie, yes you are! The best birdie in the whole wide world." He squawked, and I let him go before he pecked me to death. He definitely would never be a therapy animal, that's for sure. He was very much like a cat, only more of an asshole.

Once we had recovered enough to dry our eyes, Luke handed me my take-out container. "Sorry breakfast didn't really work out."

I accepted the container and nodded toward my place. "Wanna come in and eat?"

He shook his head. "Naw, you've had enough excitement today. You go rest. You okay if I catch up with Tamicka and look over the books?"

It was as if he splashed a bucket of cold water over me. The comradery, the laughter, the knowing looks. They didn't mean anything. He was here for the shop. "Sure, that'd be fine." I hated how unsteady my voice sounded. "But you don't have to ask. You're more the owner than I am."

"In name only. You know this is your shop, Reeses. And I want to help you try to save it."

I nodded and lifted my container, backing away. "Thanks for breakfast."

"Anytime."

I turned and made a beeline for my front door. I could feel his eyes on me the entire way, which made me walk faster and faster until I was nearly running. I needed to eat, nap, and then Google how not to be hung up on your ex's brother, especially when he was going to ruin your life.

CHAPTER SIX

EDIE'S TIP #27: TIMING IS EVERYTHING. JUST ASK
YOUR TIMING BELT

SUNDAY WAS my favorite day because the shop was closed and my mother was at church then brunch, leaving the morning hours blissful and quiet. Sergeant Cornflakes was curled up on a pile of rags I had in the corner as I worked under the hood of my beautiful Camaro. National Public Radio's *Car Talk* podcast played at full volume.

I paused my work, listening to a caller describe her car trouble like man trouble. I snorted. "It's your fuel pump!" I called out to the radio. The show had been in reruns since 2012, but I still liked to pretend they could hear me.

"Really? I would've said transmission."

I screamed, jumping high enough to hit my head on the hood and knocking a wrench to the ground with my elbow. The loud clang made my rooster squawk, feathers flying everywhere. Both of my hands went to my chest, trying to put my heart back inside. "Jesus, Luke! Warn a girl!" I bent over and put my hands on my knees to catch my breath.

He was struggling to contain his laughter as he approached with his hands in the air as if I were a skittish animal. The hosts of the

45

show seconded my opinion, saying the issue was probably with her fuel pump. Luke pointed at me. "And that's why you're the best mechanic I know."

I play-kicked his shin and he put his arm around my shoulder, placing his hand on my neck to bend my head toward him. He ran his fingers over the tender spot that had just hit metal. I would hit my head every day if it meant having him touch me like this.

"You're not bleeding, so that's good," he said. "I think if you needed stitches, they would have to shave your head." I poked him in the side and he jumped away, laughing.

I pulled off my gloves and narrowed my eyes. "How'd you find me?"

He put his hands in the front pockets of his faded jeans. They were perfectly sculpted to his hips and thighs and—

Edie, down girl.

"Process of elimination. It's Sunday morning, you're agnostic, and you're avoiding your mother. You wouldn't be at church or brunch, the bakery is closed, and you didn't answer your doorbell." He shrugged, smirking.

I nodded and pursed my lips. "Yeah, okay. I'm easy." Luke smirked as I tossed the rag onto my workbench. "Want some coffee?" I held my breath as I walked past him, not trusting myself. If he smelled good, it would go to my head and I had a feeling this was a business call.

"Can you supply it intravenously?" He followed me a little too close and his scent wrapped around me.

Him.

Shut it, brain.

I dug through the cabinet, locating the good stuff Tamicka had ground yesterday and loaded the machine. Closing my eyes, I inhaled the rich scent. Luke made a choking sound and my eyes flew open. His dark gaze was locked on my face, his eyes even more green than usual.

Heat went up the back of my neck and I spun to face the cabinet and pulled down two mugs. Tired of the pot taking so long to fill and needing something to do with my hands, I expertly switched it out for a mug, then the second one. Without looking directly at him, I held one out to Luke. "Sugar and cream are down on the left."

His hand wrapped around mine as he took the mug and didn't pull away for a long moment. My entire body pulsed awake and my eyes met his. He was too close again. All I would have to do is lean forward, just a little bit, and our lips would be touching.

Remember how well that went last time?

My brain was great at dashing all my hopes and dreams like that.

Letting out a long breath, I sidled over to the sugar and grabbed a packet, carefully ripping it open so sugar didn't fly everywhere. That happened way more often than I'd care to admit. "So what has you in the shop on a Sunday morning?" Steeling myself, I glanced over at him.

He was leaning against the counter, sipping his coffee and staring at a grease spot on the floor. "Outside of the few spots on the floor, this place is immaculate."

My eyes widened in confusion. "Yeah…"

"Most shops I've been in are filthy."

I let out a humorless laugh. "Grandpa would haunt the shit out of me if I left his shop dirty. Are you kidding me? I can practically hear him rolling up the newspaper just talking about it."

Luke chuckled. "Just like my dad and the sound of his belt." He took a gulp of coffee and I shamelessly watched his Adam's apple move. Why was that so sexy?

"Have you seen him since you've been back?"

He shook his head. "Nurse said he wasn't having a good weekend and to try in a few days."

I nodded. "I'm sorry."

He shrugged. "Anyway, I spent some time going through the books." He looked over at me. "Why didn't you call me?"

"And tell you what? We are in trouble? What were you going to do from…wherever you're living now?"

He crossed one booted foot over the other. "Home base is in North Carolina, but I'm usually on the road."

"Still doing disaster recovery?"

"Yep." He looked down at his feet.

I took him in, still trying to recognize this stranger over the man I had known my entire life. He looked worn down, tired in a way sleep wouldn't fix. His nails were short but ragged, as if he had chewed them down. His stubble had grown in so much, it was becoming a beard.

T-shirts used to hug his broad shoulders and chest from years of staying in perfect shape. Now his shirt drooped, a small hole in the collar. *What happened to you, Luke?* I hopped up on the counter and rested my arms on my knees. "Why do you need the money?"

He didn't answer, just closed his eyes for a long moment.

"Gambling? Addiction? Shopping habit? Losing a bet on an alpaca race?"

He smirked. "What exactly is an alpaca race?"

I shrugged. "I don't know, but it sounds lovely."

He glanced over at me. "I always forget how much I've missed you until I see you again."

His admission did something funny to my chest, as if he cracked it open and put a flapping bat inside. This banter needed to stop immediately. "Luke, seriously, why do you need the money? What's so important that it can't wait?"

He shook his head, his face going blank. He was shutting down. "You know I wouldn't force my hand unless I had to, Edith. And I have to."

He used my real name, meaning he was serious. There was no arguing with that. "What do you make of the books?"

"You and Will split, what, eight months ago?"

I nodded.

"Business has been steadily declining since then. You need to make cuts."

48

I pushed the heels of my hands into my forehead. "I know. I know you're right. But...fuck."

"At the rate you're going, you'll be out of business by next winter."

I let my hands fall to my lap. "Does it even matter? Even if I sold the Camaro and used all my savings to advertise, I still wouldn't make the money in three weeks."

He looked chagrined. "I know," he whispered.

Tears stung the back of my eyes. "Listen, I'm going to get back..." I pointed to my Camaro. "I do my best thinking under the hood."

He nodded. "You do."

"She's almost running."

"I can't wait to take a ride in her."

I hopped off the counter and put my hand on his arm. "I'm sorry for whatever's going on. It must be hard." As I spoke the words, I knew they were the right ones. Whatever brought him back to this town he'd sworn off, whatever put the dark circles under his eyes, was the real demon.

His hand covered mine before I could remove it. "I lost a friend."

"I'm sorry about your friend." I put my other hand on top of his and squeezed.

He nodded, his hair brushing against mine. "Me too."

Disengaging my hands, I pulled away, immediately feeling the loss. He was the one person I wanted to turn to for comfort, but he was the reason my heart was breaking. "Seriously, Luke. I'm working on a solution."

"I hope so, Reeses," he said. "Because I don't know what to do."

CHAPTER SEVEN

EDIE'S TIP #11: IGNORING THE CHECK ENGINE LIGHT
WORKS ONLY UNTIL YOU'RE STUCK ON THE SIDE
OF A DESERTED ROAD IN A THUNDERSTORM. WE'VE
ALL SEEN THAT HORROR MOVIE.

THE BEAUTY of wearing makeup was that I rarely cried with it on. Mascara running down your face or smeared eyeliner was not a professional look. And it was damn expensive. I was not going to waste all this excellent makeup on an angry cry.

Anyway, I was determined not to shrink under Danny Fallon's assessing glances. I dug my stubby nails into my palm. This guy had cheated off me in biology and now he was deciding my livelihood. Maybe I should've said yes to that date back in high school. Dammit sixteen-year-old me! Way to not think ahead.

"Ms. Becker—"

"Danny, I've known you since first grade. You can call me Edie."

He folded his hands in front of him, his too-big suit coat bunching at his shoulders. "There's no way we can give you a business loan. You're already paying off a substantial personal loan. If we gave you more money, you couldn't afford the payments." He pushed a piece of paper across the desk. "This would be your new estimated monthly payment if we approved the loan."

My vision went hazy for a moment. That was a really, *really* big number. I put one hand on the edge of the wood laminate desk to steady myself, determined to make it work. Somehow. "Okay, but if I were to get the loan, I'd save the shop. I could advertise more—"

He leaned back in his chair, the squeak cutting me off. "Sixty percent of this town was born here, and the other forty percent have been here for years. They all know where your shop is, Edie. Advertising isn't going to fix this. All of the franchises in a twenty-mile radius disappearing would fix this."

My leg was jiggling with nerves, and I pressed both palms on the desk as if pushing against it would change his answer. "I'm going to lose my house and my shop without the loan."

Danny leaned forward. "I think you should consider selling. It's your best option. Buy yourself one of the new condos your mom's building and live a maintenance-free life."

I gave up being professional and pressed my forehead to the desk. Danny's great-grandfather was one of the founders of this town and had opened this credit union nearly a century ago. Silly me for thinking he'd understand. "Danny, what would you do if you were going to lose the credit union?" When he didn't answer, I looked up to find him frowning at me.

"I'd go work at another one, I guess."

Well, I guess I kind of asked for that answer. I stood up slowly, making sure I was steady on my feet. I now regretted wearing heels, but I had wanted to look as professional as possible. For no good reason, apparently. After saying goodbye with a sweaty handshake, I escaped into the gray morning.

The misty rain immediately clung to my skin, as if the sky were trying to hold back tears as well. An angry gust of wind barreled into me, shoving my hair into my mouth and up my nose. With a growl, I yanked the hair tie off my wrist and shoved my hair into a low bun. Today was definitely the Monday-est of Mondays.

BY THE TIME I had changed and turned on my computer, it was already 10:17 am. Perth, Australia was twelve hours later than here, which meant catching my dad was unlikely. Taking a deep breath, I opened Skype and looked at my contacts list.

I fell into my chair when I saw he was still online. After selecting his name, I pressed the call button and crossed my fingers. He answered with a grunt, his bright yellow oxford shirt was the first thing I saw, followed by his smile—Jami's smile.

"Edith!" he said with genuine excitement. "How's my baby girl?"

I blinked back tears, wishing he was across the table from me, not across the world. "Hey, Dad. You're pretty dressed up for ten at night."

He looked down as if he'd forgotten what he was wearing. "Just got off a business call five minutes ago." He lifted up his leg to reveal plaid flannel pajamas. "Don't worry! I haven't gone to the dark side completely."

I smiled. "I would never assume you did."

He stared at me for a long moment. "What's wrong, Edie? Why are you calling me on a Monday morning? Why aren't you at the shop?"

I opened my mouth to talk and burst into tears. Covering my face with my hands, I leaned into the desk and let his soothing noises wash over me. I wanted to bury my face in his shirt while he rocked me back and forth like he had when I was a kid. But I hadn't been in the same country as this man for five years and counting. The realization made me cry harder. "I m-m-miss you," I managed.

"I miss you too. But that's not why you're crying and it's kind of freaking me out. The last time you cried was 2017 when Dodge discontinued the Viper."

I laughed a watery laugh and struggled to take a deep breath. "Don't remind me." I hiccupped. "Seriously underrated car."

"Start at the beginning." He leaned forward, putting his chin on his hand.

So, I did. Mom getting engaged and announcing it at Kristy and

Sam's wedding, Luke returning home, the shop, the bank, the money, all of it. "Dad," I whispered. "I don't know what to do."

Dad nodded seriously for a long moment. "I know that you're attached to the shop. You lived and breathed that place from the second your grandpa put a tool in your hand." He chuckled to himself. "Your first word was car."

I smiled. "I was an awesome kid."

"Yeah, you are." His face grew soft, and for a moment, it didn't feel like there was a computer screen between us. I could almost feel his beard burn kisses on my cheek and smell his sweet aftershave.

Then a knock at his office door jolted us out of our shared moment and the thousands of miles poured back in between us. Elaine, my dad's second wife, walked in with a sleeping toddler on her shoulder. "Oh, sorry, Edith!" she whispered in her soft, accented cadence. "Sean, I'm going to bed. G'night!"

"Night, Elaine," I said, shifting in my chair. I had never met my half brother, Tom, and I didn't know if I ever would. Traveling to Australia was a bucket list item for sure, but not something I could afford. Dad had gone down there on a business trip right after he and Mom divorced and he never came back. His trips home went from every month to every year to almost never.

I guess I couldn't blame him. Who'd want to fly almost thirty hours one way to hang out with adult kids and a bitter ex when you had a new, loving family at your fingertips?

Dad walked over to his new wife and whispered something too soft for me to hear before kissing her goodnight. I looked away to give him privacy until he sat back down and spoke again. "Listen, Edie. Your mom and I got pregnant young, too young. The ink was barely dry on our diplomas when we got married. Cynthia..." He let out a sigh and leaned back in his chair, crossing his ankle over his knee. "Her bags were packed for California before that first pregnancy test came back positive. She wasn't even planning on finishing high school in Grenadine."

He shifted, his chair squeaking. "I think she feels like she missed her true calling as an actress and she's taking it out on you."

I shoved my hands through my hair. "Even though Jami was born first? Thanks, Mom," I sneered. Not that I wished this on my brother.

He put his hands up. "You don't have to complain me. I divorced her for a reason." He yawned but quickly covered it with his hand. "Sorry, it's late. Edie, your mom is that same lost little girl who saw that plus sign. She always needed external validation and her relationship with her dad was rocky at the best of times. She's never forgiven him, and therefore will never forgive you."

I shook my head. "I don't understand how they disliked each other so much yet he loved me to the moon and back."

Dad gave me a sad smile. "Your grandpa once told your mom she was a surprise baby and Cynthia didn't take it well. Dottie had already had two miscarriages and a really hard pregnancy with Mary. They had just opened the shop and were struggling. You got the good years with your grandparents, but your mom didn't. Cut her some slack, for both your sakes."

"But does she have to marry my ex?" I groaned. "I slept with him and now he's going to be my *stepdad*. I'm living a real-life soap opera."

He sighed. "Yeah, that's a little messed up. But listen, if marrying Will is a way to get her off your back, I say good riddance." He looked at me, holding my gaze. "You always have a bed down here, okay? I'll even buy your plane ticket."

"Thanks, Dad," I whispered. Maybe if I sold the shop, I would go down there for a little while. Clear my head and meet my new brother.

He yawned again. "It's bedtime for your old man."

"Dad, wait..." I swallowed hard. I couldn't believe I was about to ask him this for the first time in twenty-five years. "Do you have money that you could loan me? I promise I'll pay you back with interest."

He shook his head. "Baby girl, pack up your favorite memories in the house, sell everything, jump on that motorcycle, and travel. See the world. Come see me. Fix cars along the way. Find a new life for yourself that's not drowning in resentment and baggage."

"Dad..."

He stood up and leaned down so his forehead was huge on my screen. "Love you!"

"Love you—" I was cut off by the screen going dark. I stared at it for a long while, my emotions swirling like they always did after I talked to my dad. I wasn't sure what I'd thought he would say.

I shoved my chair away from my desk and put my legs over the armrest, sending myself spinning. I was out of ideas. Sitting upright before I made myself puke, I stopped in front of the bookcase tucked next to the computer. Amid the romance novels, the mystery series, and the gluten-free cookbooks were my old photo albums.

Grabbing a yellow and blue paisley one off the shelf, I sat on the floor and opened it to the center page. I smiled at the picture of me standing on a bumper helping Grandpa check the oil in a car. I couldn't have been more than six or seven. My fingers trailed down the photo, missing my mom's dad so much it hurt.

Each page of the book brought a new memory of him. Us in the auto shop, us at a car show, me in a brand-new pair of coveralls that were rolled up eight times. My mom must have *loved* that.

I flipped to the end, where eleven-year-old me was smiling at my birthday cake with a model Camaro on top. Grandpa stood behind me with his hands on my shoulders, which meant Grandma was probably taking the picture.

Mom had her arms crossed and her hip jutted behind me and Dad was talking to Mario, Luke and Will's dad. Jami sat next to me, his finger already in the frosting, and Will was playing a video game on a handheld device.

But it was Luke I couldn't stop looking at. He was on the other side of me, smiling at me. I'd had his undivided attention, even then. I told that bat inside my chest to stop flapping its wings.

Flipping through more pages, I started looking for Luke. He was always standing close to me, smiling. Camping trips, school rallies, family picnics. There he was.

When I reached the final page in the book, I came face-to-face with our prom picture. He was wearing his dress blues and I was wearing a white sequined tutu dress that I had worked my ass off to afford. So much sparkle. He had his arm around my waist and I had my hand on his chest, both of us smiling.

Holy crap, it looked like a wedding picture. We stared into each other's eyes as if we had a secret. As if we were in love. The only thing missing was a ring on my left hand.

"Nope!" I yelled, closing the book and shoving it off my lap. "Nope, nope, nope. Not gonna happen." I rolled onto my back, then to my knees, pushing myself off the floor. It was time to get dressed for work and ignore the one fact that was beginning to push its way through decades of denial.

I was crazy about Luke.

CHAPTER EIGHT

EDIE'S TIP #4: SOMETIMES THE ONLY CURE IS TO ROLL WITH THE WINDOWS DOWN AND THE RADIO UP. PREFERABLY SOMETHING EMBARRASSING SO YOU GET WEIRD LOOKS.

DESPITE THE EMAIL CAMPAIGNS, business had only ticked up 8 percent. In any other situation, I would be ecstatic. Now I didn't know what to do. I spent every spare minute over, under, and inside my Camaro and still hadn't figured out a clear path forward. Only one way was clear—the one with the giant For Sale sign.

Giving up on car therapy, I turned my attention to the garage doors. I knew it was silly to replace the door opener when I was probably going to sell, but I had already done the other two. My anal retentiveness was having trouble not doing the third.

I grunted, trying to remove the clevis pin and ring fastener from the bracket above the garage in bay three. I had done this with no trouble in the first two bays last week, but my head wasn't in the game. The pin and fastener fell to the concrete below and the chain opener tried to crash down with it. "No you don't, you asshole!" I snapped, practically hanging off the ladder.

Chieka bolted over from her tire change and grabbed the opener, setting it safely on the ground. "Whoa, careful! You okay?"

Face hot with anger and embarrassment, I climbed down the ladder. "I'm sorry, I'm fine. Just have a lot on my mind."

She looked me over. "Like how Luke is back in town and he can't stop finding reasons to come by the shop?"

I opened my mouth to argue with her just as Luke's truck pulled into the parking lot. Chieka turned to me, lifted her brow, and went back to fixing her tire without another word. I stood frozen in place as he walked in looking better than a 1935 Mercedes-Benz 540K. Which was to say, absolutely delicious.

He made a beeline over to me and lifted his phone up. "You're absolutely terrible at answering your cell."

I lifted my eyebrows and looked around me. "I was on a ladder. Even if I knew where my phone was, which I hope is in the office, I wouldn't've answered it. Why didn't you call the shop?"

A smile touched his lips. "I did, but Tamicka said you were on a ladder and couldn't talk."

I lifted my hands up. "Well, there you have it."

He looked at the wreckage from the garage door and the giant box next to me. "Why are you replacing the garage door opener?"

"The chains were causing trouble. I'm changing them all over to steel reinforced belts."

He looked at me for a long moment before stepping closer. "Why are you putting money into the shop right now?"

I took a step closer to him. "Because I already bought this, and I needed something to take my mind off..." I waved my hand in the air. "I'm thinking about it so hard, I can't think of an answer."

He grabbed my shoulder and spun me toward the back door. "I'm stealing Edie. She'll be back," he yelled to Chieka. He gripped my arm and dragged me forward. "What you need is a break." Sergeant Cornflakes looked up as we passed, but made no effort to disengage himself from his tire bed.

"You really suck at this guard rooster thing," I grumbled.

Tamicka leaned out of the office. "Take your time with her, young man. She needs some TLC!"

"Over the line, T-Money!" I called back.

"I'm with T-Money!" Chieka yelled.

"You're all fired!" I warned.

"I'm due for a vacation anyway!" Chieka quipped.

With a growl, I pulled my arm away from Luke's and stomped ahead of him on the path to my house. "Why must you encourage them? They already think we're sleeping together." He didn't respond, and I looked behind me as I shoved my key into my lock. "What?"

"Would sleeping with me really be so bad?" he asked, his voice gravelly.

I blinked and took a deep breath, warning the bat inside to stop fluttering. "I didn't say that. I'm just getting all the flak and none of the perks." Oh holy hell, did I just flirt? "Anyway, what are we doing here? I have garage doors to uselessly repair."

I shoved open the door and let him walk ahead of me. Like I had been doing since I started working in the shop, I kicked off my boots and slipped into the laundry room off the living room. Closing the door, I slipped out of my work clothes, depositing them in the basket, then scrubbed my hands and arms until they were red.

I gave my face a quick rinse before grabbing the yoga pants and T-shirt I had left waiting there this morning. I still smelled like the shop, but at least I was clean. When I walked back into the living room, Luke was running his hands over the fireplace mantel. I took a moment to light my favorite scented candles around the room.

He turned to face me. "Usually when a woman is lighting scented candles around me, something else is about to happen."

I blinked up at him, wide-eyed, just realizing how it must look. "No! I mean...I'm not trying to make a move." He was laughing at me, clearly teasing, but I couldn't stop the words from falling out of my mouth. "Grandma hated how we smelled after a day in the shop." So had Will. He wouldn't even kiss me until I showered.

I had spent my entire life trying to cover up the dirt and fumes that clung to me every day; it was kind of a hard habit to break now.

Anyway, my friend Dawn had made these hot chocolate candles and I was totally okay with my house smelling like chocolate.

Luke walked over and rested his hands on my shoulders. "Edie, every time I fill up my gas tank, I think of you." I flinched. He squeezed. "That's not a bad thing! It's an Edie thing. You don't need to cover it up. I like you just the way you are."

My heart did a shimmy and a shake, and I didn't know what to concentrate on first. If he thought of me every time he filled up his tank...that was at least once a week, right? And he liked me just the way I was? What did that even mean? I had so many questions...and now I was humming Bruno Mars.

He laughed softly, then released me, looking around. "You've done some work."

I smiled so wide, my face hurt. "Want the grand tour?"

"Absolutely."

We started in the living room, where I had restored the fireplace mantel and refinished the wood floors that had been underneath thirty-year-old carpet. Luke bent down and ran his hand across an area of the floor. "I love this finish."

"I went with polyacrylic, which I know has its downsides to polyurethane, but I like it better. And less off-gassing."

He nodded and followed me through the dining room, which was now painted a beautiful deep teal. "Taking down the wallpaper wasn't the hard part," I told him. "It was the glue underneath. I can tell you which parts Grandpa did and which parts one of his guys did. But I finally got it sanded and painted."

Luke's hand trailed the edge of the bright white wainscoting that covered the lower half of the wall.

We walked into the kitchen and he let out a low whistle. "Double ovens? Butcher block counters? Breakfast bar? Be still my Grinch-heart."

I laughed. "It's been a slow process, but perseverance, craigslist, and builder sales have made it possible."

"You did this all yourself?"

I shrugged. "Jami and Sam helped. So did YouTube and years of hoarding Grandpa's advice."

He walked over and bumped my shoulder with his. "Reeses, this is amazing. It's a different house."

"It's just a little updating. My memories are still in its walls." I had lived here almost my entire life, moving back in after my parents divorced. Then I'd taken care of my grandma and then Grandpa while they were sick. When they were gone, staying here and taking over the shop had just been natural.

The thought of leaving it all made my stomach twist with nausea. "Luke, please. Don't sell."

He stepped back as if I'd burned him. "I came over to show you something." He pulled out his phone and navigated to the shop's business page. Tamicka usually monitored it, but I really needed to check it more.

"This was shared from Instagram to Facebook. It has eighty views." He pressed play on a video and Bridget Gentry, a local single mom who was in the shop last week, started talking. She'd had a faulty barometric pressure sensor and since I had just fixed three similar model SUVs with the same problem, I knew exactly what to do.

"If you're tired of the 'boys club' atmosphere of auto shops, I cannot recommend Edie's Auto Shop in Grenadine, Michigan enough! It's run by Edie Becker, who is an amazing woman! I had taken my car into three other places, like a novice, even though I live right outside Grenadine. It was awful. Not only could they not replicate the issue I was having, but they tried to upsell me constantly."

She shifted her recording, so the auto shop sign was in view. It must have been a Sunday morning since the shop was closed. "Edie and her women were finally able to figure out why my check engine light kept coming on despite the fact that I had just had the transmission and fuel pump replaced. They are a bit pricier than the big chain shops, but so worth it. Five stars!"

The video cut off and I had a stupid smile on my face. "She was so cool."I looked up at Luke, whose face was very close to mine. In fact, his entire body was close to mine. We were arm to arm and I savored every single inch of it.

Taking a controlled, deep breath, I moved away before I did something stupid...like lick the side of his face. I really needed to stop being in the same room as him, alone. Maybe invest in a blindfold when he was around. Naw, the blindfold wouldn't help. Unless, I was tied to the—

Edie. Focus.

Luke stepped back and tucked his phone in his pocket. "Maybe start giving twenty dollars off a bill if people leave you a video review and tag the page. Do you have Instagram?"

I shook my head. "No, but it can't be that hard."

He looked at me, bewildered. "You're like the only twenty-five-year-old I know without social media."

I scoffed. "Please. There's at least three of us. Besides, you don't have Instagram."

"Ah, but I do." He smiled, and my stomach flipped.

Was I missing out on pictures of Luke? "Wait, what?"

He pulled out his phone again and opened the app. His account came up with a picture of a rock as his avatar and zero posts.

I elbowed him. "You have no pictures. That doesn't count, dork."

"Hey, now. I follow people!"

"But you don't post. Glad I'm not missing much."

Luke touched his head with his index finger. "But the shop is missing. I can help set it up, add some pictures. You can even schedule posts! We'll make you your own hashtag. #EdiesAuto."

I studied him, trying to understand what was going on. "You're making it really hard to not like you right now, and I really want to hate you because you're trying to take away my shop."

He studied his boots. "I'm not trying to take away your shop. I'm trying to make good on a promise I made to help a friend, and in order to do that, I need cash." He looked up at me, his eyes pleading with me to understand. "It was never supposed to hurt you."

He let out a long breath. "Now, come on. Where's your computer? Let's set up this account."

I thought about being alone with Luke and my computer. In my room. "Uh...it's not working right now," I lied. I can't be blamed. If he walked into my bedroom, my clothes would instantly evaporate. *Poof!* Then I'd be naked. Bad idea.

Great idea! my brain said. *Get naked. Get him naked!*

Luke narrowed his eyes for a moment as if he could tell I was lying, then pulled out a stool at my counter. "No problem. We can do it from my phone."

I sat down next to him, trying not to touch any part of his body. This worked until he said, "You should do this. Learn the interface." Then he put the phone in my hand, our fingers brushing. The jolt shocked me, and I dropped the phone on the counter with a muttered apology.

I was hyperaware of him the entire time we set up the account and wrote the bio. He followed it up by uploading a picture of me from earlier this week that was saved on his phone. I was standing next to his truck, tool in hand, sassy smile on my face.

Luke had a picture of me saved on his phone. Somehow this felt important.

He showed me how to use some fancy app to repost the video from Bridget onto the shop's page. "There," he said. "Just post every day, add a hashtag, and let's hope you get an uptick in business!" He set the phone down between us.

I leaned in sideways and wrapped my arms around his shoulders. "Thank you." I amazed even myself when I didn't bury my face in his neck and inhale deeply. I deserved a medal.

His hand wrapped around my forearm. "You're welcome, Reeses. Now you just need a phone that knows what apps are."

It took all my strength to pull away. "Ugh, that sounds horrifying." I put my head on my hand and looked at him for a long moment. He seemed...unsettled. "Is this why you came over?"

He smiled and shook his head before reaching into his back

pocket and grabbing his wallet. He pulled out a piece of paper that had been folded and refolded a hundred times and tossed it onto the bar in front of me. "I was going through some of Dad's stuff packed away in Will's basement. Found that and thought you'd want it."

The paper was as soft as cotton. I unfolded it carefully as if it would disintegrate if I moved too fast. Flattening it out, I leaned close to read the faded cursive words. My grandpa's words.

January 23, 1973

Dear Mario,

Dottie and I were so thrilled to hear President Nixon announce that the war is over! She cried and even I wept in relief. I thank God that you are coming home. I wish my brother Gerard was still alive to hear this news.

Everything is still the same in Grenadine as it was before you left, waiting for you to return. It will be hard to adjust to civilian life, although I'm sure you're ready to get out of the jungle. I know I was. How terrible that we are six years apart in age, yet we fought in the same war?

Working on cars helps me cope. I've been doing more and more work around town because no one wants to drive twenty miles to get their oil changed. I'm happy to do it. It keeps the nightmares at bay.

We should open that automotive repair shop we talked about. I've got some money saved and Dottie wants to leave teaching so we can start a family. I'll need your help running the shop. What do you think?

This can be a legacy we pass on to our children. Something to be proud of that doesn't involve bloodshed. Something we built with our bare hands.

I wish you peace and safe travels, my dear friend. I can't wait to see you.

Your Friend,
Edward

I didn't even realize I was crying until Luke stuck a napkin in front of my face. "This is amazing," I whispered, afraid talking too loud would somehow make the letter disappear.

He stood, and an unfamiliar emotion flickered in his eyes. Regret? "We have to find a way to save the shop so you can hang that letter on the wall." He ran a hand through his hair and tugged. "That shop was their refuge." He looked at me. "It's yours too."

I nodded.

"I wish I had a refuge," he admitted so quietly, I almost thought my ears were playing a trick on me.

"I..." I started, swallowing hard. "You're always welcome to come work with me if you ever leave disaster recovery. You know almost as much about cars as I do."

He shrugged, refusing to meet my gaze. "The thing about that letter...I dunno. I was so mad at my dad for so long, you know? So angry that he could cheat on my mom, that everyone could just pretend our family was normal and okay and that I wasn't some adopted mistake. But maybe it's because Dad was never normal and okay again and Mom just did the best she could."

I nodded. "Grandpa had demons, too. Sometimes, when he didn't know I was there, I'd see the edge of them."

Luke looked out the kitchen window and into the backyard, where my chicken coop sat at the front of a half acre of lawn, butting up to trees older than me. The grass needed mowing soon, but I just hadn't gotten around to it.

"Mower still in the garage?" he asked. "Code the same?"

"Yep."

"Get back to work. I'll take care of your yard."

"Luke," I protested. "It's okay. Jami promised to do it this week."

A loud buzzing startled me, and I jumped, looking down at the counter. Luke's phone was ringing, and a picture of a beautiful woman flashed across his screen. My chest was heavy as if I had just run three miles.

He snatched the phone and answered. "Hey there, Alice May."

I debated getting up to give him some privacy, but I couldn't bring myself to move.

"Yeah, I'm coming home in a few weeks." He paused, listening to her. "Miss you too. What'd the doctor say?" Still on the phone, he gave me a low wave and started walking out the back door.

Questions I wanted to ask bounced around my head. Who was Alice May? Did he miss her, or did he *miss* her? Why was she at the doctor?

Was she Luke's friend? Girlfriend? I rubbed the heel of my hand against my chest, trying to ease the tightness. I needed to get back to the shop and talk to Tamicka about social media advertising. I needed to figure out how to make the money to save the shop. I needed to get my hands dirty.

I needed to start an Instagram page called "How Not to Jump Your Ex's Brother Who Will Only Break Your Heart."

CHAPTER NINE

EDIE'S TIP #33: A FRIEND IS SOMEONE WHO SHOWS UP WHEN YOU BREAK DOWN ON THE SIDE OF THE ROAD. A BEST FRIEND IS SOMEONE WHO HELPS YOU KEY YOUR EX'S CAR.

THE AMBUSH HAPPENED RIGHT after I sank onto the couch after a long, hot bubble bath. They were lucky I had a tank and shorts on and wasn't lounging around naked. Of course, I didn't typically lounge around naked since clearly too many people had copies of my key.

Kristy barged in with a take-out bag from Ray's. "We brought dinner, *chica!*"

Sam followed with Jami bringing up the rear. Sitting up, I eyed them all suspiciously. "You have Ray's, Sam doesn't come to movie night, and Jami is carrying a carton of ice cream from Mr. Moos. Who died?"

They all exchanged a look and Sam said, "I told you me being here was a dead giveaway." He spun on his heel and followed Jami into the kitchen.

"You're the one who wanted to come, babe!" Kristy called after him.

She dumped the food on my coffee table and sat next to me on the couch, sorting through the take-out containers. She handed me a plastic fork and container labeled "Edie." I flipped it open to see my favorite—spinach lasagna. I set it down and stood up, hands on my hips. "Ray only makes me gluten-free lasagna on my birthday, and once right after I called off the wedding. That's it."

She held her hands up. "I may have called him earlier."

"Why?"

"He was already making it."

"James Joseph!" I yelled. "Get in here right now and tell me what the hell is going on!"

Sheepishly, he walked back into the room with my mail in his hands. He tossed the local daily paper and a magazine on the floor under the table and held out...I didn't even know what it was. The most atrocious thing I had ever seen.

"Ew, what is that?" I asked, leaning in. "Is it alive?" It was like a piece of burlap and a pile of lace had been stuck together with a hot glue gun. Pieces of lace hung off the card with dangling, heart-shaped beads. "What is even happening right now? How did this go through the mail? I have so many questions."

Jami came to sit on the other side of me and I instinctively leaned away from the thing in his hand, still not sure what it was. He shoved it in front of my face and I saw my name was burned into a thin piece of wood stuck to the lace-burlap monstrosity. "Miss Edith Doreen Becker."

There was only one person, besides Jami when he was mad, who used my full name. I stared at him. "It's from Mom?"

"Open it," he said.

"Can I choose option B?"

He shoved it into my hand and I flinched, waiting for it to start sucking on my flesh. A solid ten seconds later, when it hadn't moved on its own accord—at least I didn't think it had—I flipped it over and found a flap sealed with wax. "There's a lot of...crafting," I said diplomatically.

"You know Mom doesn't really know how to craft," Jami

muttered. "Remember when she volunteered to make the costumes for the Christmas pageant?"

Kristy, Jami, and I all sucked in a breath. "Who knew that Baby Jesus had a robot arm and seven glow necklaces?" Kristy asked. "I sure didn't."

After peeling back the wax seal and opening the envelope, I pulled out an invitation. A wedding invitation. A wedding invitation for my mom and my ex's wedding. I rolled my eyes so hard, I swore they got stuck for like three seconds. "For fuck's sake, how many times do I have to tell this woman no?!"

I looked at Jami. "It's not a secret they're getting hitched. I appreciate all the effort you went through, but I'm fine."

"Read it," Jami ordered.

I frowned and concentrated on the super flowery calligraphy. "Blah, blah, blah, request the honor of your presence at their wedding on September..." A rock lodged in my throat. My eyes scanned down the page as my hand started shaking.

Same day.

Same time.

Same venue.

Will was still going to get married on our wedding day. He'd just replaced the bride. Without a word, I stood up and walked over to the fireplace. After opening the flue, I grabbed the lighter on the mantel and set the invitation on the grate.

There was silence as I watched the flames lick around the non-recyclable paper. I wanted to put the envelope in too, but I figured the burlap and lace would stink up the place. I should bury it in the backyard with some salt, maybe burn some sage. Make sure it wasn't cursed or something. That'd be my luck.

When the invitation was nothing but ash, I reached for my lasagna and a fork and took a big bite. I knew therapy eating wasn't a good coping mechanism, but sometimes carbs and cheese were the only things that could heal a wound.

"I don't even want him back!" I admitted through a mouthful of pasta. "I didn't love him like I should, and he definitely didn't love me enough. But why does she need to make everything about her? Why am I the one she constantly steps on to make herself feel better?"

Kristy put her arm around my shoulders. "Let it all out."

I shoved another forkful in my mouth and chewed for a long moment, then swallowed. "I'd rather eat." I pointed my fork at Sam. "If you want to make yourself useful, pick a bottle of wine from my wine rack and bring me a giant glass."

He jumped up and escaped to the kitchen, clearly uncomfortable. I put my head on Kristy's shoulder. "Poor Sam. You should've warned him."

"I tried. He seemed to think our family was worth all the drama."

"Well, *you* are."

When Sam brought in two bottles of my favorite wine, I knew it was not going to be a sober night. To be fair, I only bought the good shit. Life was too short and money was too precious to buy mediocre alcohol.

I tossed my phone onto the coffee table. "Before I drink an entire bottle of wine, someone needs to take my phone away. I do not need to be drunk texting *anyone*." I glared at said phone, annoyed that I hadn't heard from Luke all day today. Or all day yesterday.

Pfft. Whatever. I hadn't checked my messages for a good hour. Well, a half hour. Maybe more like fifteen minutes. I may have also texted myself from Chieka's phone earlier to make sure my messages were working.

If a tree falls in the forest and no one is around to hear it, does it have to admit it kept restarting its phone to make sure it was working? Asking for a friend.

Kristy snatched up my phone and tried to unlock the screen, pouting when she couldn't remember the passcode. "Not fair. Who are you trying not to drunk text? Does his name rhyme with Yuke?"

I glared at her. "I don't know who you're talking about."

Jami snorted. "Sure. He wasn't the guy whose face you were sucking in your Camaro."

Kristy and Sam shouted "WHAT?" at the same time. I threw a pillow at Jami's face.

"It wasn't like that!" I explained. "And I need way more wine for this conversation."

Sam poured a good amount of wine in a coffee mug and handed it to me. "I get the phones if you're drinking. There's no drunk texting on my watch."

Kristy rolled her eyes but handed him her phone. "Who am I going to drunk text? You're here."

He gave her an exasperated look. "Your mom, your sister, Aunt Cynthia, MY mom, and sister...maybe even my dad. I don't know. You talk to everyone." He looked at me. "I swear my family talks to her more than me."

I looked between them and pursed my lips. "Yeah, that sounds like Kristy."

Jami tried to hide his phone between the seat cushions and reached for a bottle of wine. "Nope!" I shouted. "Pony up! No phone, no wine."

Sam shrugged. "You heard the boss."

I tilted my half-empty mug at him. "Thank you. I like you. Welcome to the family." I started singing "We Are Family."

He chuckled as Jami handed his phone over after sending a quick text.

"The things I do for my sister," Jami grumbled.

"Whatever, loser." I studied him for a long moment. "Who, pray tell, are you texting?" He took a glass from Sam and took a swig to avoid answering. "Wait, why do Kristy and Jami get fancy glasses and I have a mug?"

Sam smirked. "Because you can fit half a bottle in that mug and it has a handle."

I snapped my fingers and pointed at him. "Good man."

Kristy elbowed me. "Spill."

I rolled my eyes. "I got a bit tipsy at your wedding for...obvious reasons." Kristy and Sam both winced. "Luke was at my shop when I came home. We were chilling in my Camaro and I read the situation wrong. Very wrong. The worst way wrong."

"How wrong was that, again?" Sam teased.

"So wrong." I sighed. "I tried to kiss him, and he absolutely did not kiss me back."

Kristy and Sam both hissed. "Ouch," he said.

I held up my mug in a toast and then drank it dry.

The night progressed with all of the carbs and both bottles of wine. Chieka showed up after an hour with gluten-free brownies. "I just got the invitation and thought you may need these." She held up the plate of deliciousness. "They're out of a box, but they're full of chocolate, so how bad could they be?" She handed me the box to review the label.

She squeezed onto the couch, making Jami take a chair in the corner. The brownies were still warm, and the ice cream melted slowly over top of them. After confirming they were indeed Edie-safe, I proceeded to eat them in mass quantities. I was well into a food coma when the words started spilling out of my mouth. "I paid for the deposits on the venue, the band, the caterer. Will told me he tried to cancel, but they were nonrefundable. I was so caught up in wanting it all to be over, I didn't fight him. It was just money, and I had enough. He promised he'd pay me half, but..." I lifted my hand and let it fall.

Kristy was lying on my thighs. "It's been eight months and you haven't gotten it back yet?"

I shrugged. "You know how I feel about confrontation."

"That's messed up, Eds," Chieka said, pointing her spoon at me.

I scraped the bottom of my bowl, my lips turning down as I realized I had eaten all of my brownie. "Yeah. Could use that money right now."

Jami held his hand out. "Sam, give me my phone. I need to make a few calls."

Sam shook his head. "Love you man, but no way. Not until you sober up. I have three sisters. I know how these sessions go down. You get all riled and wrapped up in the drama and you say shit that can't be unsaid."

I looked at Kristy. "You picked that." I reached out and fist-bumped her. "May we all be so lucky." Murmurs of agreement faded away as we all turned back to the television. We were streaming *The Great British Baking Show. Queer Eye* had been vetoed on account of *feelings.* No one wanted to cry tonight.

"You know what really gets me?" I said, pulling everyone's attention away from Norman's lavender meringue. "He's marrying my own mother at MY venue reserved with MY money. I bet he's even using the same photographer! He should pay me back. I mean, a few grand isn't going to put a dent in the one hundred seventy-five thousand, but it's a start."

Chieka and Kristy both looked at each other, then at me. *Oh shit.* I hadn't told them. I groaned and grabbed a throw pillow and put it over my face.

"What are you talking about?" Kristy asked at the same time Jami said, "You mean one fifty?"

Kristy choked on air. "What the hell?!"

I kept my face buried in my pillow and motioned for Jami to tell the story. So he did. Chieka sat up on the couch and shook her head, staring at me. "Why didn't you tell us?"

"Because I'm the boss. It's my responsibility to figure it out!" I countered.

She poked my shoulder. "No, you idiot. We're a family. You're practically the only family I have stateside. We need to fix this."

"Let's talk about this when we're both sober, okay?" I pleaded. I couldn't handle another emotional topic tonight.

She studied me for a long moment. "Okay, Edie-Bean. When we're sober."

Sam groaned and grabbed a phone off the dining room table and tossed it to Jami. "Man, it keeps buzzing and it's driving me nuts. You're probably sober enough to deal with it."

We all turned to look at Jami whose ears were red. "James Joseph, who is texting you?" I asked.

He cringed. "Well, fourteen are from Mom."

"How many calls?"

"Three."

"Ugggggh. Can I divorce a parent at twenty-five? Is that a thing?"

Kristy looked terrified and gripped my arm, her fingernails digging into my skin. "You can't leave me alone with Aunt Cynthia. I thought you loved me."

I yanked my arm free. "I do love you. I'll take you with me."

"Deal," she said. Sam was pursing his lips, clearly trying not to say anything else. Kristy caught on. "Spill it."

He shrugged. "Just gonna say, there were more than fourteen texts."

Jami bit his lip and dipped his head. I clapped loudly. "You met someone!"

My brother laughed. "It's eerie how you can do that."

I waved my hand. "I've always been able to read you. Who is he? Where did you meet him?"

"The coffee shop. And we had a date last night."

Sam covered his ears milliseconds before Chieka, Kristy, and I screamed. He really did fit into our family perfectly. I dove off the couch and wrapped my brother in my arms. "I'm proud of you," I whispered, knowing how special this moment was. "You haven't dated anyone since..."

"Yeah." He gave me a quick kiss on the top of my head. "It's terrifying."

I nodded but didn't say anything. It was too sad of a story for tonight. "Let's finish the brownies and pass out."

CHAPTER TEN

I HAD GOTTEN ready for bed before I allowed myself to check my phone. It's not like anyone texted me anyway. Wow, defeatist language much?

When I saw eight missed texts and one missed call, all from Luke, I promptly fumbled my phone and it hit the floor, then my foot kicked it under my bed. Because, of course. The phone started vibrating, alerting me to an incoming call.

I dove under my bed, thankful I had recently vacuumed up the alternate universe of dust bunnies and cobwebs, and checked the screen. *Him.* I stood up and quickly checked out my reflection in the full-length mirror, making sure that I looked cute enough to answer. Universal truth—a girl had to be cute when answering a call from the guy she liked.

I cleared my throat as I slid my finger across the screen, trying to be casual. "Hey, Luke. Everything okay?" I put my hand on my hip, then immediately took it off. Why didn't I know what to do with my hands while I was on the phone? What did I do with them usually? Oh God, I couldn't remember.

"I've been trying to get ahold of you all night! Are you okay?"

I blinked. He sounded angry. I pulled the phone away from my face and checked to make sure I was, in fact, connected to Luke. "Uh, I'm fine? Sorry, no phones allowed on Besties' Night."

He sighed. "I'm outside your house. I got worried."

"Why?" I was genuinely flummoxed.

He paused for a beat. "Did you check your mail today?"

Oh, that. "Yeah...hence the impromptu Besties' Night."

"Oh. That's good." Was I imagining it, or did he sound...left out? "Well, never mind. I'll just—"

"I'll be right down. Hang tight!" I slipped on a hoodie over my tank and shorts and shoved my feet into my cat slippers—because I was twelve at heart—and glided down the stairs. When I opened the front door, Luke was sitting on my front step, head hanging.

He straightened, his eyes raking over me as I walked out and sat next to him. "You really okay?" His eyes went down to my feet and he smirked. "Never change, Reeses."

I bit my lip and looked away from him. "Yeah. A bit shell-shocked, but okay."

Luke bumped his knee against mine. "I can't believe your mother would actually want to take your place like that. She's such a diva; wouldn't she want her own date?"

I shrugged. "She's the one who picked out the venue and stuff. I just wrote the check. It probably should've been a sign that I didn't even care where or if we got married. I just wanted it to be done."

He nodded. "Yeah. Typically, even if you hate wedding planning, you should want to be married."

"Who knew, right?" I laughed without humor.

We were both looking up at the sky, silent except for the hum of cicadas weaving through the muggy evening. I was on the edge of town at the end of a street. The lights from Main Street were just far enough away to not block out the stars. It was one of my favorite things about this property, and something I didn't appreciate nearly enough.

He shifted on the step and lifted up his invitation. "I'm thinking we should do an exorcism and bury this in the backyard with holy water and a few crosses. I'm afraid I'll accidentally summon a demon if I open it."

I threw my head back and laughed. "I burned mine earlier. It was freeing!"

"Do you have a lighter?" He reached out his hand.

I shook my head. "Luke, you should go to that wedding. It's your little brother."

He studied me for a long moment. "He hurt you."

Those three words knocked the breath out of me. "I hurt him, too," I admitted softly.

He nodded and tucked the envelope into his coat pocket, pulling something else out and offering it to me. "They're gluten-free, I checked."

My eyes went from the orange package of peanut butter cups to his face. It was such a small, simple gesture, but it vibrated all the way to my core. I was so used to being mocked for my dietary restriction except by my closest friends and Jami that I was thrown off. "Thank you," I whispered, taking them. Years of memories, of sitting on the porch like this eating candy, washed over me.

He smiled, and that damn bat was back in my chest. Focusing on the package, I pulled out the first cup and shoved the whole thing into my mouth. I moaned at the delicious goodness coating my tongue. "Ohmygod," I mumbled through a mouthful. "Itssogood!"

Luke threw his head back and laughed, and I stared. It took years off his face. His laugh was even sexier than his voice, all gravelly and contagious. I concentrated on swallowing so I wouldn't choke. That was not the way I wanted to go, although I couldn't fault it as a last moment.

I pulled the second cup out and held it up to him.

He shook his head. "They're all yours."

"Nope. I can't do another one. I already had brownies and ice cream and lasagna. If I eat anything else, I'll cry." My stomach gave a kick in agreement. I was going to have to eat salad the rest of the week to lower my blood sugar.

He raised his eyebrow but leaned forward and parted his lips.

I didn't breathe, couldn't breathe, as he bit the candy in half. His warm lips brushed against my thumb and forefinger and a jolt went down my arm and straight to my stomach. Well, this was not how we used to eat candy, but I didn't mind. He chewed, swallowed, and licked his lips. My eyes followed his every movement as he leaned in again and took the rest of the morsel in his mouth.

I bit my lip, stifling a strangled gasp. His tongue brushed my fingers, licking the chocolate off. His eyes met mine as he pulled away, and I was pretty sure I was hallucinating. Because he was looking at me like he wanted to lick more than my fingers.

My nipples hardened at the thought and I was super thankful for my baggy hoodie. His hand went around my wrist and he brought my fingers to his mouth again. He paused for a moment, giving me the chance to reject him, but I definitely didn't want him to ever stop looking at me like that. He sucked my index finger into his mouth, sweeping his tongue over my skin.

I breathed in sharp through my nose, putting my forehead against the side of his head. "Luke," I cried softly, so many thoughts in that one word. *We can't do this. You're just going to leave. It'll make everything too complicated. You're trying to take away my home. I would give anything to kiss you. You'll break my heart. Stay.*

And Luke, being Luke, heard every unspoken word. He released my finger and moved so we were forehead to forehead. "I'm sorry," he breathed, mere centimeters away from my mouth, the scent of peanut butter and chocolate hovering between us. "I should go."

I nodded, so close my bottom lip touched his top one. "You should."

A loud *cocka-doodle-do* rang out, shattering the moment. For once, I was extremely happy about Sergeant Cornflakes's insomnia. Luke stood quickly and jumped off the steps, stopping with his back toward me and his hands in his pockets.

"I'm sorry. I crossed a line."

"It's..." I cleared my throat, flinching at the croak that came out. "It's okay."

He stared down at his feet for a moment. "Goodnight, Edie."

"Night, Luke." I watched him walk down the path to his truck. It took all my willpower not to run after him and invite him inside. My body throbbed in protest, but my heart beat an extra beat as a thank you. She'd been broken enough this year.

CHAPTER ELEVEN

EDIE'S TIP #5: CUPHOLDERS ARE TO CARS LIKE
POCKETS ARE TO WOMEN'S CLOTHES. THE MORE,
THE MERRIER. SURE, YOU CAN STICK YOUR STUFF
IN YOUR BRA, BUT THEN YOU'LL HAVE A LUMPY
THIRD BOOB.
#ISUPPORTCUPHOLDERSANDPOCKETS

I HONESTLY THOUGHT the banging was in my head for a solid two minutes. But then the doorbell started ringing in long bursts, as if someone was leaning into it. I muttered a half-formed curse word and rolled over to nab my phone from the nightstand. I missed and fell out of bed, my legs tangled in sheets.

"Seriously?!" I yelled, untangling myself and grabbing my phone. It was only six thirty. In the morning. Apparently, there was one of those in the morning too.

The phone in my hand started buzzing and I growled as "Mom" flashed across the screen. Choosing to ignore the phone, I stomped out of my room and down the stairs screaming "COMING!" over the din.

I yanked open the door with a death glare. "Someone better be dead!" I yelled into the still morning. The sun was just peeking above the horizon, making my mom's blonde hair glow red. The humidity was already thick, and I instantly broke out into a sweat.

Mom flung her hand to her chest as if offended. "Edith, is that any way to greet your mother and sister?"

I almost retorted, "Oh you finally realized you had another daughter?" But I didn't, because Clementine didn't need any more baggage. Stooping down to the sleepy little girl who had just celebrated her sixth birthday, I opened my arms and she walked right in. The stuffed rabbit she carried with her, Muffy, snuggled into my neck and I smiled. I'd missed this girl. "Missed you, Tina."

She snuggled into me deeper. I looked up at my mother, who was looking at her phone. "I need you to take her today. I'm knee-deep in wedding stuff and, you know how it is."

I frowned and pulled back, kissing Tina on the forehead. "Why don't you take Muffy and go sit on the couch? I'll be right there, and we'll make breakfast!"

Once she was safely inside, I stepped out onto the porch and closed the door. "What the hell are you doing on my doorstep at six thirty in the morning?!"

My mom's eyes grew large. "Watch your tone of voice."

"Mom, cut the shit. I was up late, I'm exhausted, and I have to work today. I can't take a day off to babysit. You only get her two overnights a month. Why the hell aren't you making more of an effort?"

She took a step back, clearly not expecting this reaction. To be fair, I had never been so direct with her. It was like the burning of her wedding invitation had forged my backbone into steel. Or maybe she'd secretly tried to curse me and it had backfired. Either-or.

She sputtered. "Her father had to go out of town and needed to switch days. But I already have a meeting with the caterer and a dress fitting today. You know how much time wedding planning takes."

I threw my hands up and let them slap my legs. "I can't believe you're standing here right now and saying that."

"Please, Edith. I'll come get her at three."

I looked back at my door and thought of the little girl inside. How many times had I sought refuge in this house? How many times had

Grandma and Grandpa taken me into their arms at the ass-crack of dawn? They had saved my life, and now I needed to be there for my sister.

"Fine. I'll watch her." My mom opened her mouth to say something, but I held up my hand to silence her. "I'm doing this for her, not for you. No child should feel like a burden to their parent." She tried to talk again, but I shook my head. "Next time, you give me no less than twenty-four-hours notice, or I will call her father and talk to him directly."

"You have no right—"

"He was my stepdad, Mom. We still talk on holidays. I'm sure he'd love to hear from me more."

We stared at each other and she broke first, like I knew she would. I held her freedom in my hands. "She's picked up by three," I demanded. I always got a rush of people in the afternoons and these days, I needed all the work I could get.

With a solemn nod, I spun on my slipper and marched back into the house.

AFTER STUFFING our faces with chocolate chip pancakes—she didn't seem to mind that they were gluten-free—we watched the Disney Channel while I braided her hair. When I had finished, Tina ran her hand along her braids and bent her head backward to give me a huge smile. She poked my ribs, which spurred a tickle fight until we were both laughing so hard, we were gasping. We collapsed back onto the couch, our heads together.

"I know I'm supposed to like hanging out with Mom, but I like you better."

I grabbed her hand and squeezed. "Why don't you like hanging out with Mom?"

She fisted the bottom of her dress. "She makes me wear dresses and I can't climb any of the giant trees in her yard."

I nodded. "Yeah, I can see why that would be sad." I clenched my jaw, resolving to be a good, older daughter. "But maybe that's 'cause she can't climb trees with you. Is there anything she likes to do that maybe you would like to do too?"

She shrugged. "I dunno. She's always trying to dress me up or having Special Mommy Time."

I frowned. "Special Mommy Time?"

"It's when she and Will go into their room and lock the door." She picked at the hem of her dress. "I'm not allowed to knock unless it's an emergency."

I cringed. Did six-year-olds know about sex? Should I be giving her a sex talk? And seriously, my mother couldn't wait until after she went to bed on the rare occasion Tina was there? She went to bed at like eight or something. "Uh..." *Smooth, Edie.*

"I know what they do. Mom talked to me about it when Will started coming over. I thought he was *your* boyfriend, but Mommy says he's *her* boyfriend."

I twisted the end of her braid around my finger, trying to figure out what to say. "He used to be my boyfriend, but we didn't love each other like we should. So we broke up. Mom and Will love each other the right way. That's why they're getting married."

"He was going to be my brother and now he's going to be my daddy. It's weird. Do I have to call him Daddy? I already have one."

I choked on air. This was possibly the most awkward conversation I'd ever had. I pursed my lips. How did I answer this? *Why yes, it IS weird.* "What do you want to call him?"

She shrugged. "Will? Stepdad Will? Mr. Will?"

Stepdad Will? Geez. "You're a big girl and get to decide what to call him. Next time you're hanging out alone, you can ask him what he thinks. You can decide together." She nodded seriously, like a woman in her thirties instead of a little girl. "You know, Mom and your dad still love you even though they're not together."

She nodded. "I know. Daddy says that. He says Mommy's a man-eater, but she won't eat me because I'm a little girl. I asked him if that made her a zombie, but he just turned red and didn't answer."

I opened my mouth to respond and found that I couldn't. I had zero responses. What the hell did you say to that? My cell phone started ringing and I had never been more thankful for an interruption in my life. I leaned forward to nab it from the coffee table. "Edie," I answered.

"I know you got roped into babysitting," Chieka rushed out, "but I need Doctor Edie."

I looked over at Tina. "You up for hanging out at the shop?"

She sat up and nodded with a gap-toothed grin. "Yeah!"

"Give me five and we'll be there." Looking at Tina's pink dress, I pursed my lips. "Okay, ten." After hanging up, I jumped off the couch and started upstairs. I had to have something too small that she could change into. "Come on, pip-squeak! Let's get you out of that dress."

FIFTEEN MINUTES LATER, I had added a hole in a belt and made a T-shirt into a dress for Tina. Her pink frilly concoction was safely hanging in my closet. She held my hand and skipped down the path to the shop, rattling on about Sergeant Cornflakes.

"When I'm a vet, do you think I could have a pet rooster, too? How did you get yours? Does he have a wife? Or maybe a husband? Daddy told me sometimes men fall in love with other men. Do roosters fall in love with other roosters? Do roosters taste the same as chickens?"

I was simultaneously mentally high-fiving her dad, Gabriel, for being open about homosexual love, while also regretting how much sugar I'd given her before this errand. I did this to myself, didn't I? I was the one who put the chocolate chips in the pancakes. Next time it would be fresh fruit and oatmeal.

She kept up her questions until we reached bay one, barely

breathing in between bursts. Thankfully she didn't seem to expect me to answer because I had no idea if roosters could fall in love with other roosters. I was going to have to Google that later.

As soon as Chieka saw us, she rushed over. Tina's eyes widened as she followed her progress. "Wow, you're pretty," she said. "Daddy says only pretty girls can work at Sissy's shop."

I mentally retracted my high five for Gabriel. I didn't hire based on looks. I hired based on talent, skill, and willingness to learn.

Chieka crouched in front of Tina with a smile that could light the way in a snowstorm. "Hi Clementine, my name is Chieka."

Tina stuck out her hand and the older woman shook it. "It's nice to meet you, Chieka. Your name is weird like mine. We should be friends." She said it with such seriousness, Chieka and I both started laughing.

"My name is Japanese," she explained. "Which is why it seems weird."

Tina nodded sagely. "My name is a fruit. That's why it IS weird."

I loved this kid. When I finally recovered enough to take a deep breath, I raised my eyebrows and looked at my employee, a silent gesture for her to tell me what was up. If I opened my mouth again, I was going to lose it.

"Ellen Lencroft is in town visiting her grandkids. She's been having trouble with her car since she left Colorado and stopped at two mechanics. No one has a clue."

I looked around the waiting room and found the older woman sitting there with a worn novel in her hand. Ellen was in her mid-sixties but looked like she could be forty. Her tawny complexion was nearly flawless. Only the gray peppered throughout her hair gave her age away.

When she saw me walking toward her, she put her book down and smiled. "Edith Becker, you are a sight for sore eyes!" She stood and opened her arms.

I bent down and kissed her cheek. "Ellen, it's been years! How's Mateo? How's the family?"

She smiled and nodded. "We're as good as it gets! Health is hanging on, maybe not the hearing so much but it just means I don't hear Mateo snore." She touched her ear. "Probably why I'm losing my hearing anyway!" We laughed as she looked down at Tina. "Who is this precious girl?"

"Ellen, you remember Clementine? My half sister."

Ellen looked between us in apparent shock. "No way. I haven't been away that long! There's no way she's the little girl you carried in your backpack when she broke her leg because you both wanted ice cream."

I wrinkled my nose. "She's too big for my backpack now." Tina's smile grew huge and she bumped into me, her normal shy move. "Every time I see her, she's grown half a foot!" Of course, I barely saw her thanks to my mother and her ridiculous custody agreement. At least we had Skype.

Ellen, Tina, and I sat down as Ellen showed me pictures of her kids, grandkids, and her new dog, Prince. I could feel Chieka hovering nearby, awaiting orders, but this was important. If Ellen wanted impersonal service, she could go somewhere else. I had known Ellen all my life and loved hearing about her family.

"Tell me about your car," I finally asked. Out of the corner of my eye, I saw Chieka step closer.

Ellen pointed to the diesel pickup truck in bay one. "We bought this off of one of Mateo's pickleball buddies after we upgraded our camping trailer, and you know my little gas truck just couldn't keep up. Anyway, it started shuddering on our way here!"

"Describe the shuddering to me. Did you notice any patterns?" Ellen described her drive, the truck's symptoms, and her visits to the last two shops.

Chieka approached to give me a rundown. "There're no codes and I couldn't replicate it. I can't find a vacuum leak. I changed the spark plugs. Oil change, synthetic, a thousand miles ago. Looks pretty clean. She said she had the fuel pump replaced at shop number two and is afraid she needs a transmission."

I tapped the front of my forehead, my mind running different scenarios. "She said the worst part of her trip was Colorado...I think we're too flat. I wonder if it's a misfire..."

Chieka clapped once in excitement. "I'll grab the laptop and oscilloscope."

I turned back to Ellen. "Let me run some tests. I have a theory. If you want to order anything from Ray's, let Tamicka in the office know. They'll deliver." I turned to Tina. "You wanna go color with my friend Tamicka?"

Ellen tutted me. "We were going to go find Sergeant Cornflakes and see how his day is going." She chuckled, standing up and reaching for Tina's hand.

Ellen had babysat me when I was a kid, so I was confident in her ability to watch Tina. Without having to worry about my sister underfoot, I got to work hooking the machine to the truck's engine and grounding it to the battery. Once the laptop was up and running and the bay door was opened, we started the truck and studied the computer, and waited.

And waited.

And...waited.

The thing about intermittent engine backfires was that they were intermittent. In any other aspect of my life, this would make me crazy. But in my gut, I knew I was right. It was just a matter of time...

"There!" I said. "There's the misfire. Just dropped completely."

"Number four injector," Chieka concluded, looking over my shoulder. "I'm on it." We high-fived.

"Rosa!" I called, and my youngest employee poked her head out of the employee lounge. "Got time for a detail and wash today?"

She nodded. "On it!"

Adding on complimentary services was never a good way to make money, but Ellen was an important part of my childhood. She got the works.

Ellen, Tina, and I walked up to Ray's to get the food and went back to the shop to eat in the employee's lounge. In this room, you could tell the shop was run by a bunch of women. A real wood table with non-folding chairs, white cabinets, a light-blue subway tile backsplash, and fingerprint-free stainless-steel appliances made it feel like home. The microwave and dishwasher were starting to show their age, but I'd replaced the fridge only two months ago.

When I finished eating, I rotated out with Chieka and double-checked everything on Ellen's truck. In the meantime, Rosa had made it shine. "Ellen!" I called, walking over to the waiting room. "We're finished."

She listened while I explained what the problem was and how we'd fixed it. I answered all of her questions, then directed her toward Tamicka in the office for payment. "I added in the car wash and detailing on the house. Don't you dare tell her to charge you for them."

She swatted playfully at me. "You're not going to be able to pay the light bill if you keep doing stuff like that."

I shrugged. "I've got candles."

After a goodbye that was a bit more emotional than I expected—I really needed to take her and Mateo out to lunch before they headed back West—I looked over at Tina. "You ready to go back to the house?"

She shook her head. "Can you show me some car things?"

I blinked, surprised. "Uh...sure! Let's grab you a step stool!" It should have occurred to me to set an alarm or to put someone on alert to watch out for my mother, but sometimes I did stupid things. Especially when my Camaro was involved.

CHAPTER TWELVE

"SEE how this is different than the new car we looked at?" I asked Tina, who was sitting in the driver's seat, pretending to drive.

Tamicka knocked loudly before rushing into the Camaro bay. The look on her face was a warning. I glanced at the clock on my workbench. *Shit.* Three fifteen.

"What the hell are you doing with my daughter?" our mother screeched.

I helped Tina out of the car and turned her to face me. "Thanks for spending the day with me! You were the best helper." I kissed her cheek and used the movement to wipe some grease off her face with my thumb.

"I have been knocking on your door for fifteen minutes and you're not answering your cell phone! I cannot believe that you would be this irresponsible. Bringing a child—*a child*—to this shop is dangerous!"

I straightened and hardened my face. "Are you serious? You let me hang out here with Grandpa from the moment I could hold myself upright!"

"Yes, and look how you turned out." She stomped forward in high heels that were so shiny, I could see my face in them, and snatched Tina's hand from mine. "Come on, Clementine." She gasped. "Where is your dress?!"

"I hate that dress," Tina mumbled. "It doesn't have pockets."

My mom put her hand to her chest and pointed a talon at me. "You did this. You put these thoughts in her head." She stepped forward, tugging Tina with her. "Just because you grew up to be like Fiona, Franky, whatever the hell her name is now, does not mean you get to shove your poor fashion choices down my child's throat!"

Oh, *now* Tina was my mother's child when it was convenient for her argument. Cute. "Okay, there's so much to unpack here. First of all, Franky is a transgender man. His pronouns are he/his/him. Stop calling him Fiona and using female pronouns. Second of all, regardless of their lifestyle, people are allowed to dress outside of stereotypical gender roles. Third, I'm wearing jeans and a tank top. This isn't Victorian England. I can show my shoulders."

"No wonder William loves me better."

Punch to the gut. I was surprised I didn't double over. Not because I cared about who Will loved more than me—I hoped he loved the woman he was going to marry more than me because what we'd had wasn't enough. It hurt because it was my mother saying it. The woman who was supposed to love me and charge into battle for me, not against me.

I swallowed hard, refusing to cry. I wouldn't give her the satisfaction. "I'll go get Tina's dress." I walked right past my mother, pausing only to squeeze my sister's hand, and raced up the pathway to the house.

Mom had stripped Tina the moment she got through my front door and was scrubbing her in my powder room. "You smell terrible," Mom complained. When she was done making sure her baby was clean, she grabbed the dress from my hands and shoved it on a wincing Tina. Mom clapped her hands twice. "There, that's better."

"Mom—" I started.

She held up her claw—I mean hand—to silence me. "No.

Clementine is the last chance I have to raise a proper woman who isn't an embarrassment." She grabbed Tina's hand and started to the front door. "My friend Amy is going to call you about my bridal shower. Make sure you answer."

Then she slammed the door her father had built without looking back.

CHAPTER THIRTEEN

EDIE'S TIP #21: I, TOO, LIKE TO NEGOTIATE HOW
LONG I CAN KEEP THE GAS LIGHT ON BEFORE I FILL
UP. HOWEVER, THIS PROBABLY ISN'T THE BEST LIFE
CHOICE...

I'M NOT ashamed to admit that I cried when my mom left. I cried because I wanted the mom I saw on television shows, the one who had family dinners and supported her children. I cried because I kept reacting to what she said. I cried because I hated the daughter I'd become. I cried because she called me an embarrassment.

For the first time, I saw the silver lining in leaving this shop and this house behind. I could leave my mom, Will, and all this drama. It meant being away from Kristy, Jami, and my shop girls, but we could still get together. Luke could have his money; I could have a life without the dragon.

I ran to the alcove in the hall where Grandma kept her old house phone, pens, and pads of paper. The phone had been long disconnected, but I still kept it exactly the same. Grabbing a pencil and pad, I started to write down what I would need to replace before I sold the house. The front door—that would come with me.

The stained-glass sconces in the hallway that Grandma had purchased in Italy on their twenty-fifth-anniversary trip. The dining room chandelier that was my great-grandma's and had survived the journey from Poland. The staircase banister my grandpa's brother helped install right before he was killed on tour in Vietnam.

As I went through every room in the house, my heart grew heavier and heavier with each step. These walls contained generations of love, heartbreak, and memories. How could I leave this all behind? Even if it meant leaving my mother.

Sitting on the edge of my bed, I covered my face in my hands, wishing I could talk to my grandpa right now. He'd know what to do. He'd hand me one of his perfect chocolate chip cookies—which I had never been able to replicate—and tell me everything was going to be alright.

I pushed my fingers back through my hair and my gaze landed on my bookshelf. Amid the colorful paperbacks and knickknacks was a framed photo of my grandparents with Luke's parents as they cut the ribbon the day the shop opened. I slid off the bed and walked over to it, picking it up.

Luke's dad, Mario, was the only one in the photo still alive, but his memories had been locked away after a series of strokes. Still, the need to see someone who'd known my grandpa as well as I had was overwhelming. After rushing through a shower, I braided my hair, threw on fresh jeans, and headed to my garage to pull out the one vehicle that could make me feel better—my motorcycle. Henry had done a custom paint job on her a few years back, and she glittered purple and orange in the afternoon sun.

With my matching purple helmet in place, I revved the engine and took off. Mario was at a memory care facility thirty miles away. It was one of the fancy ones that had its own city within the grounds. I knew how much Will paid a month, but he didn't even flinch. It was one of the few decent things about him.

The drive was just what I needed. The speed, the wind, and the sunshine restored me. By the time I pulled up to the facility, I was feeling more like the Edie I wanted to be. After signing in and being issued a visitor's badge, I made my way to Mario's room.

His door had a license plate hanging from a ribbon with his name on it, but nothing else. No pictures, drawings, or Fourth of July decorations. I briefly thought about the photo on my bookshelf and wondered if I should bring a copy over. I'd have to ask his nurse.

I hesitated before knocking, not sure if it was even still appropriate for me to see him. But I didn't break up with him, I broke up with his son. If he didn't want to see me, I'm sure he'd tell me.

Squaring my shoulders, I knocked three times. A garbled "Hello?" came through the thin door, and I turned the knob and stepped inside.

The room was a small studio apartment, maybe five hundred square feet. A small kitchen was to my left with a tiny table and two chairs. The wheelchair accessible bathroom was to my right, which had two access doors—from the front hall and from the bedroom. Everything was beige and gray, and I instantly longed for the bright colors that their family home had boasted.

"Hi, Mario," I said cautiously, approaching the thin man in a wheelchair near the couch. He was watching golf and struggled to pull his focus away. "Remember me?" I asked as his milky gray eyes washed over me.

He lifted his hand and motioned me to come toward him. He gripped my hand in both of his and held it. "Dottie, I was wondering when you were going to come see me," he said. "I haven't seen you or Edward in forever!"

I bit my lip. "I'm Dottie's granddaughter, Edith. Remember me?"

He patted my hand again before motioning for me to sit down on the couch next to him. Once I was seated, he grabbed my hand again. "They tell me I'm sick. Haven't gotten to the shop. Tell Ed I'm sorry. I'll get there soon."

I swallowed hard and smiled weakly. "Of course. He's been working on the Camaro."

He smiled and leaned his head back. "Ah, that one's a beaut! Take me for a ride when it's done?"

I nodded. "I promise." I didn't actually know if I could get him in the car, but I would try my best.

He sighed and looked back at the television. "I hate golf. But there's nothing on except this and politics." He tapped his head. "I may be a little sick now, but even I know that guy is *pazzo*."

"You've got that right."

We sat in silence for a long time, watching the golfers take shots over beautifully manicured courses. I looked at the scattered frames along his window ledge, most of Will and Luke when they were kids. One of him and my grandpa in their coveralls, drinking beer. I swallowed hard and turned back to the television.

When the next commercial break came on, he hit mute and looked at me. "My sons are idiots, Dottie. You gotta help them out."

A laugh escaped me, and I smiled at him. "What do you mean?"

He grumbled something under his breath. "I'm afraid William will grow up to think he needs money to be happy. There's no shame in working in the shop. I put food on the table. Just because I can't buy him a brand-new video game every time it comes out, he thinks we're poor." He tsked. "He wants to see poor? We'll go visit *mio fratello* Angelo. Lives in one room."

I squeezed his hand. Uncle Angelo had passed away from cancer the summer before high school. William and Luke had stayed with us while Mario and Caterina, traveled back to Italy to be with him for his last weeks.

He shook his head. "And Lucas..."

My heart picked up its pace, wanting to hear what he said. "What about him?" I prompted when he didn't continue.

"I don't know when that boy is going to realize he's in love with Edith."

I stilled, my breath caught in my chest. My chest and neck grew warm. "Why do you say that?"

He lifted our hands in a sort of shrug. "He's too worried about getting out of here to realize it. I know I made some mistakes, but that boy needs to get his head on straight." He reached over and unmuted the television as the commercials ended, and refocused on the television, leaving me to deal with this bombshell on my own.

I knew I needed to take everything he said with a grain of salt, but there was a part of me that desperately wished for it to be true. His memories were intact; they were just locked into a different time period.

"Mario. When the kids take over the shop, what if they want to sell it? All of our hard work?"

He looked over at me for a long moment, then shrugged. "It's just a shop." He said something in Italian that I think meant "as long as my children are happy, I'm happy." I made a mental note to Google translate it later.

I WRESTLED SILENTLY for the next half hour with everything he'd said before the afternoon nurse came in to get him ready for the dinner service. With a hug and kiss goodbye, I promised to visit again soon. The ride home revived me a little and I swung by Ray's for a to-go salad before heading into the shop.

I needed to get my hands dirty. This weather was perfect, midseventies and sunny, and I decided to work with the Camaro's bay door open. The shop had closed an hour ago and the street was silent.

I was comfortably ensconced in *Car Talk* and rebuilding the engine when the sound of tires on warm pavement put me on alert. I eyed the crowbar near my workbench and slowly shifted away from the Camaro and toward the weapon. I knew better than to leave the bay door open when I worked in here alone, but I'd needed the sunshine today. Why did someone always have to ruin a good thing?

As soon as I recognized the stomping, I put the crowbar down, but only so he wouldn't tell everyone I assaulted him. Shame I couldn't punch him in the throat just for existing. My ex walked into the bay with his immaculate suit and a sour expression on his face.

"We're closed," I said, deadpanned.

"I still own part of this shop, Edith," he returned, his gaze narrowing. "My fiancée told me how you treated her and Clementine today."

I blinked. What in the actual fuck was going on? "Okay, first off—"

"I don't want to hear it! How could you bring Clementine to the shop today? She's young and impressionable."

I threw my hands in the air. "Mom showed up on my porch this morning without warning. Guess what? I have a job. Someone has to run this shop because Lord knows neither you nor Luke plan to!"

"And that's another thing! If you had to work so badly, why am I hearing from the nurses that you went to visit my dad today?"

I frowned at him. "I broke up with YOU, not your family. I went to see him because I wanted to. Your dad is the only decent adult left in my family!"

"He's not your anything! He's mine!" He slapped his chest. "You are the most selfish woman I know. You only think about yourself and cars."

"Get out of here. I don't want to see you."

"Just do us all a favor and sell the damn shop, Edith. No one trusts a female mechanic anyway. Go to college, get a grown-up job, and start being an adult."

I eyed the crowbar again. I bet I could get one good swing in.

"You don't get to try to weasel your way back into my family because you miss me. I found a *real* woman who makes me happier than you ever did."

This time, I didn't hesitate. I reached for the crowbar and held it up. "Get. The. Hell. Out. Of. My. Shop."

William turned on his two-hundred-dollar shoes and stomped back out the way he came. I threw the crowbar after him and enjoyed the loud clatter it made as it hit the pavement. I wiped my hands on a towel and grabbed my phone. I hit my cousin's number and held my breath as it rang and rang.

The moment before it went to voicemail, she answered, out of breath. "You're calling me and not texting me! What's wrong? What can I do?"

I took in a shuddering breath, but couldn't manage more than a squeak.

"I'm just closing up the salon," she said. "Give me twenty and I'll be there. Do you trust me?"

I nodded, even though I knew she couldn't hear it.

"I'll assume you're nodding. Be there soon."

CHAPTER FOURTEEN

EDIE'S TIP #34: MY BEST PICKUP LINE IS "YEAH, I'M TOTALLY CHECKING OUT YOUR TAILGATE."

I SHOVED another bite of Edie-safe tacos in my mouth as Kristy finished doing my hair. Eating with my eyes closed was a challenge, but I was willing to get a little guacamole on my face. I was full two tacos ago, but they were my favorite food, so I had just unbuttoned my jeans and kept going.

Kristy put down the curling iron with a clunk. "Okay, wipe your hands off and cover your eyes. I'm spraying you." I took a deep breath and held it, covering my face. "This is a texturizing hairspray. I'm leaving it for you."

Once it was finished, she waved her hand in front of my face, her bracelets tinkling together. "Voilà! Now, give it a minute or two to dry, then run your fingers through the curls. It'll give you badass, beachy waves."

I let my hands fall to my lap. "I like how you say that like I know what that means." She rolled her eyes, then poked me in the side. "I'm kidding, I'm kidding!" I laughed, shoving her away. Despite not wearing makeup or doing my hair often, I knew a few things from my mother's obsession with "looking feminine" and Kristy's ministrations.

When she pulled back, one of my curls caught on her sleeve, and I saw pink. I gasped, jumping up from the chair and running to my bathroom mirror. She had cut several inches off but still left it long enough to weigh down my locks. But the best, most amazing part, was my light blonde hair was now pastel rose pink.

I turned to look at her when she walked in, then turned back to the mirror. My eyes filled with tears and I shook my head. It was perfect. A color I'd always wanted but wasn't brave enough to try. I'd always been so afraid of what my mom or Will would say.

"Say something," Kristy said.

"It's perfect," I whispered, pulling at a curl. "How'd you know?"

"I pay attention. It's my job." She wrapped her arm around my waist. "When I showed you a pic of Michelle with her pink hair, you talked about it for weeks! You weren't ready for pink hair then, but you are now."

I nodded, my hands against my cheeks. "I am now," I agreed.

She turned me toward her. "Get ready. Get makeup on. We're going out."

"Find me an outfit that will hide my taco belly," I ordered.

She rolled her eyes. "Be proud of that taco belly! But maybe for comfort, we won't go with skinny jeans." She winked at me and left the bathroom. "Tonight, we take back the real Edie! Fuck these bitches!"

I laughed and grabbed my phone and my makeup case, turned on my favorite upbeat playlist, and got to work.

GRENADINE WASN'T KNOWN for its nightlife, so Kristy and I climbed into her Camry, whose brakes I had just replaced, and took it a few cities over to a local jazz and margarita bar. My flirty black A-line tank dress, stack of rose gold jewelry, and pink hair made me feel like a new woman. This was the person I knew I was inside. I was a car lover, I was a woman, and I was strong.

We were halfway through our chocolate martinis when Jami and Chieka showed up, making gasps of shock—Chieka—and squeals of delight—Jami. They fingered my hair and toasted Kristy and called my ex every name in the book once they heard the story. I was flying high on my happy buzz and finishing drink number two when I spotted a familiar broad set of shoulders and dark hair walking toward me. My stomach tightened, and my heart started doing a triathlon.

"Oh yeah!" Kristy proclaimed, all innocently. "I invited Luke."

My mouth went dry as Luke approached, wearing a tight black T-shirt and perfectly worn dark jeans. "Holy hell," I whispered, my verbal filter clearly left in the wreckage of martini land.

Chieka let out a low whistle. "Is he walking in slow motion or is it just my imagination?"

Jami nodded. "No, I honestly think it's slow motion. There's no reason he should look this good in a plain black tee. It's not fair to us mere mortals." I kicked him under the table.

Luke smiled shyly as he approached the table. "Hey guys. Kristy told me to be here or..." He stopped midsentence when his gaze landed on me. He rocked back a step and blew out a breath. "Holy hell, Reeses, you look phenomenal."

I smiled so hard my jaw hurt. I flipped my hair a little. "Like it?"

He nodded, keeping his eyes locked on me. "Very much."

Kristy moved from my side to the empty chair next to Jami. I widened my eyes at her with a silent *way to be obvious*! Luke sat down next to me, letting the entire side of his body brush against mine. My nipples pinched and my chest hollowed out like I had just run a marathon.

Maybe it was the pink hair, maybe it was the two martinis, maybe it was my face-off with both my mother and Will, but I no longer cared how long he was in town. I wanted the man next to me, badly.

It was time for new Edie to get what she wanted.

That was assuming Alice May wasn't his girlfriend. But then

would Luke be this flirty with me if he had a girl back home? Surely not.

I really needed to woman up and ask him. Come on Edie, just ask him. Simple question. *Who is Alice May? Do you have a girlfriend? Can I suck your face?* Okay, maybe not the last one. Yet.

His arm went around the back of my chair and I leaned into him and chickened out. I knew Luke wouldn't be like this if he wasn't single. So, instead of being an adult and asking, I put my hand on his knee. His leg tensed under my hand for a brief moment and the muscle I felt under his jeans made my heartbeat thrum in my ears.

"Edie...." he whispered.

I looked at him. "I'm going to stop drinking. Just in case."

His eyes went dark and his gaze held mine. He didn't respond, but when the waiter came by, he ordered both of us a coffee. Kristy's eyebrow nearly touched her hairline, but she didn't say anything. Kristy looked at Jami for support, but he was glued to his phone. She frowned when she realized our fifth group member wasn't next to her. "Where's Chieka?"

I tilted my head toward the bar. "Talking to the band, most likely about the mechanisms that make piano keys work." She was awesome like that.

Kristy elbowed Jami. "What?" he snipped.

She rolled her eyes. "I was trying to find someone to be in cahoots with about the fact Luke just ordered a coffee for himself and Edie, but you're not paying attention and Chieka is nerding it up."

Jami frowned between us. "So? Eds loves coffee."

Kristy stared at him for a moment. "She stopped drinking alcohol..."

"Okay?"

"Because she wants to be sober..."

I smacked the table in front of her. "Stop, he's not going to get there. It's a sibling safety feature. Like a mental block."

"Seriously?" Kristy asked the table at large. The leg under my hand shook as Luke tried to cover his laughter with a hand over his mouth. Annoyed, Kristy reached over and grabbed Jami's phone from his hand.

"Hey, Kris, don't be an ass!"

She held the phone out of his reach. "Who are you texting? That guy?"

"No," he lied. I could practically see his nose grow.

I sucked in a breath through my teeth. "You're never getting that phone back now," I muttered.

"Ask her about my Game Boy," Luke said.

She shrugged, unapologetically. "I warned you. Call me a bitch, I would take your Game Boy."

Luke nodded. "A lesson I learned the first time. At eleven. Never called a woman that again."

Jami plopped his head on his arm and groaned into the table. "Fine! Fine. That guy I met? We're going out on our third date tonight."

Kristy yelled, "I knew it!" She promptly handed his phone back. He snatched it and hid it under his leg.

"Third date?!" I exclaimed, nearly spilling my coffee in excitement. "You clearly had amnesia and didn't tell me about the second one. Spill. Is he nice to you? What's he look like?"

He rested his chin on his hand and stared at me. "His name is Caden, he looks like Karamo Brown's twin, and I'm leaving the bar in ten minutes because I want to make out with him."

I let out a low whistle, because Karamo Brown was delicious.

"Caden LeBlanc?" Luke asked. Jami nodded. "Met him a few days ago when I was doing forty-five in a twenty-five."

"He's the new cop in town!" I exclaimed.

Luke nodded. "I'm straight, but I would definitely consider at least making out with that guy. He is a beautiful man."

Jami's ears turned pink and he bit his lip. "He's pretty great."

I groaned, then laughed, putting my head against Luke's shoulder. "Jami, I don't want to think about you making out, 'cause gross.

But also—" I reached out my hand for a fist bump and he gave me one.

"Thanks, sissy."

As Jami told us the story about how he and Caden met and about their first two dates, Luke's head leaned against mine. I concentrated hard on controlling my breathing. It was so easy to fall into him, to not fight against this attraction. For tonight, I was going to pretend there was nothing between us.

So when Jami kissed my cheek and told me he'd call me tomorrow, I leaned into Luke more. His arm tightened around my shoulders. Then when Kristy made her excuses to get home to Sam, I laced my fingers through Luke's. And when Chieka decided she was going home, my lips brushed the skin next to Luke's ear as I whispered, "Want to get out of here?"

He just nodded.

CHAPTER FIFTEEN

THE RIDE HOME was silent except for the "Yesterday's Country" station playing in the background. Luke had placed our joined hands on his leg before he started his truck and drove the half hour back home. Every mile ratcheted the anticipation higher and higher. Would he kiss me? Would he do *more* than kiss me? Was this all we'd ever be?

As we pulled into my driveway, the opening guitar to Taylor Swift's "Love Story" started playing. I put my hand over my face and laughed. It was too much. All I needed now was some lightning bugs to form a heart outside the window. Maybe some cherry blossom trees to shed their petals strategically around the car.

"Uh...are you okay over there?" Luke asked, a smile on his face.

I laugh-sighed. "Yep, totally cool. Nothing to see here."

"Is this a drunk-Edie thing?"

"Nope, haven't had a drop to drink in two hours." I pointed at the radio. "This song. It just..." I took a deep breath. "It has memories."

Luke's smile grew. "This song always reminds me of prom."

My breath caught in my chest and my gaze snapped back to his. "Me too."

His eyes held mine and all of the humor was gone. "You were wearing that dress—" He motioned to his torso. "It had those holes cut out in the side."

I smiled. "My mom hated that dress, but I bought it with my own money and there was nothing she could do about it." I bit my lip. "It's probably why I still have it."

His gaze grew dark and he leaned closer. "When this song came on, I had my hands around your waist, touching that skin. You threw your head back and sang every word."

I laughed softly. "Yeah, this was like my favorite song foreva."

Luke's fingers reached up and caressed my jaw. "I wanted to kiss you so bad, it hurt." He let his hand fall away. "But it wouldn't have been fair. I was only home for a few days and you were still so young."

That bat in my chest started a rave and invited her friends. I held out my hand. "Get out. Dance with me."

He watched me for a long moment before he nodded once and walked around the truck. He opened my door and helped me down, then leaned in to turn up the radio. My heart punched my ribs when he took me into his arms. This time, we danced like adults, with one of his hands at my waist, the other clasped with mine, fingers woven together.

Temple to temple, we swayed under the full moon to the song I always associated with him and that night. This was dangerous. More dangerous than just taking his pants off with my teeth, which I bet my dentist would frown upon.

His head moved, bringing our foreheads together. "Edie, we can't do this."

I sucked my lips in. "You have a girl back home, don't you?"

"It's complicated. But...no, I don't have a girlfriend. Just a friend. I wouldn't be holding you like this if I did."

I swallowed down the lump in my throat. "She the reason you need the money so badly?"

He nodded. "If I have to sell the shop to your mom, you'll hate me. I'll hate myself. But all I can think about is kissing you."

"Luke...I—" I screamed when something hit my leg and squawked. I jumped away from Luke, flinging my hand to my chest.

When it started crowing and rustling feathers, I started mentally cataloging chicken recipes. "That damn bird!" I screeched, chasing it. "You're going to make a really good chicken marsala!"

Sergeant Cornflakes flapped his wings, crowing again before running toward his coop. I was cockblocked by my very own cock. I took a deep breath and shook my head. I hated that my bird was right.

I walked back to Luke, reaching out and lacing my finger through his. I needed the skin-to-skin contact, just for a few more moments. "He was right. We shouldn't do this," I whispered. "I want you, so much. But this is already a mess. If we sleep together, it's going to make everything harder."

I leaned into him and kissed his cheek, pausing to inhale his amazing smell. "Thanks for tonight," I said. With a sigh, I stepped back and grabbed my purse from his truck.

Luke's hands were shoved into his pockets as deep as they would go as he tilted his head toward my back door. I spun on my heel and tried not to think of him following close behind.

"Listen, I..." Luke started. I gestured for him to continue as I concentrated on my feet moving toward my door. "I'm leaving soon. And..."

And I'm leaving you behind. I don't do commitment. I'll just break your heart again when I leave. I stopped walking as the last thought materialized and Luke walked right into me. "Gah! I'm sorry!" I spun around.

His hands wrapped around my upper arms, steadying me. "No, I'm sorry. I wasn't paying attention."

"My brain is trying to do too many things, like breathing and walking. Apparently, I can't do both." I rubbed my forehead, confused at my own thoughts. Had Luke broken my heart before? I had the sinking realization that he'd been breaking my heart my entire life.

I was in love with Luke.

"Fuck," I whispered. "This sucks." I looked up at him and found his eyes searching my face as if trying to solve a riddle. By the comprehension in his eyes, I figured he'd pieced something together. My grandma always said I was an open book.

"I know," he admitted quietly. "Your home is here—your life is here. It's always been, just like mine has never been."

I swallowed hard and stepped into him. "All I want is a kiss. The kiss you would've given me at prom. The kiss I will tuck away and cherish long after you leave."

Okay, I really had no idea who this person was, but it couldn't have been me. Was I this idiotic? But when his hand cupped my face, I shamelessly leaned into it and didn't regret a thing.

"Edith," he breathed, leaning his temple against mine. "I should go."

I bit my bottom lip and nodded, taking a step back. "Okay. See you...when I see you." I pulled my keys out of my purse and made a beeline for my door. My face was burning, and I was so glad it was dark. I was probably tomato red.

"Reeses," he called as I shoved the key into the lock and fumbled it open. I paused before stepping in, waiting to hear what he had to say. "I saved every email you ever sent me."

A sharp pain echoed through my hollowed-out chest. There it was. The heartbreak that was so synonymous with Luke, I had never separated them. A dozen questions rolled around inside my mouth. *Why didn't you ever write back? Why didn't you call? Text? Send a carrier pigeon? Was I so easy to forget?*

Taking a steadying breath, I called over my shoulder, "Goodnight, Luke." I was eternally thankful my voice came out even and calm. I pushed my way into the house, closed the door and leaned against it, breathing hard.

I wanted to run out and throw myself into his arms. I wanted to tell him that he was loved and cherished and belonged here with me. "Argh!" I rubbed my eyes with the heels of my hands, smearing all of my hard work. *I saved every email you ever sent me.*

I flipped off the door, like an adult, before sliding down and throwing my keys and clutch to the side. This dance between us needed to stop. I needed to move on and stop trying to...whatever I was trying to do. Make another emotionally unavailable guy fall in love with me? That sounded very consistent with my character.

I kicked off my shoes and pushed myself to my feet. I needed to get this makeup off, bra off, and get *Queer Eye* onto my Netflix. There were joyful tears to be had and I needed joyful tears.

A knock at my back door made me freeze on the stairs. I knew if I opened that door everything was going to change. I took another step up the stairs before the knock turned into a pounding.

Worried something might be wrong, I jumped down the stairs and pulled the door open, revealing Luke with eyes that burned with intensity. "Lu—"

"I saved every one of your emails," he admitted again, dispensing with a greeting. "I read them over and over again. Sometimes they were the only thing that got me through hellish days. Through the storms."

I opened my mouth to speak, but he shook his head. "I need to get this out." He leaned on the doorframe, his face bending down to mine. "Before I left the Marines, I was already doing disaster recovery. After Hurricane Sandy, we were pulling down the remains of an apartment and we found—" He swallowed hard and shook his head slightly. "You had just written to me about replacing the clutch on a '69 Alfa Romeo Spider and it was like you were right next to me."

I nodded, remembering. I'd always remember that car.

"I probably read that email fifty times that week. It made me feel like I was home." His forehead pressed against mine. "Because you feel like home to me."

All of the air in my lungs promptly evaporated. It was all I could do to stand upright. My heart did a tap dance and my stomach joined in. My hands were clutched into fists at my side, desperate to hang onto this moment. *Stay.*

"I don't know how we are going to figure this out or if it's even possible. All I know is that I cannot walk away again and not kiss you. Not kissing you at prom was something I always kicked myself for. But not kissing you right now? I would regret it until the day I die."

"Okay," I whispered, then licked my lips. "Then kiss me."

I took a step back, letting him come fully into the house. As he closed the door, his gaze moved from my eyes to my lips. "Come here," he demanded, his voice husky. As soon as I was close enough, he grabbed my waist and pulled me against his hard body. His nose brushed mine and my breathing turned shallow.

The sweet scent of him enveloped me and I happily let myself drown in his eyes. "Edith," he whispered, his lips so close, I could feel their heat. "Be my home tonight."

"Always."

And then he kissed me.

CHAPTER SIXTEEN

EDIE'S TIP #6: ALWAYS KEEP A SPARE TIRE AND A
SPARE CONDOM

LUKE'S LIPS were soft and warm, the scrape of his scruff lighting a match in my chest. We both inhaled sharply as if we had been suffocating our entire lives until now. My stomach fell through the floor. A wave of heat curled up my spine when he pulled back far enough to search my eyes.

"I should've done that the moment I saw you again," he growled before he shoved his hands into my hair and dragged my mouth back to his.

Our second kiss wasn't soft and warm, but desperate and searing. Tongues, teeth, gasps. Sparks flowed from his mouth to mine, setting me on fire from the inside. I needed to be closer. I needed to crawl into him. He cupped my ass and brought our bodies flush. I groaned at his hardness against my thigh.

If eighteen-year-old me could see me now.

Every fantasy I ever had was woefully underwhelming compared to the real-life feeling of kissing Luke. It was never like this with Will —with any man. Right now, no living room, no house, no universe existed. It was just him and me, and my heart doing a drum solo.

Him. I jolted at the thought, at the certainty from some dark corner of my brain. I wanted to yell at it, remind it that he was leaving. This wasn't forever. This was probably not even until tomorrow. This was tonight, right now. And it would have to be enough.

My heart squeezed in warning, reminding me that Luke could never be a one-night stand. We were already in too deep. *Shut up, heart.*

As if he could read my thoughts, he wrenched his mouth from mine. We breathed heavily while our hands still roamed. "We shouldn't do this," he whispered, hot against the skin of my neck as his large hand splayed against my rib cage, his thumb trailing along the edge of my bra.

My nipples pinched, begging to have his undivided attention. "I know." I ran my hands down the front of his hard chest and underneath the bottom of his shirt. My palms laid flat against his hard stomach and we both groaned. "But I'm having trouble caring about what we should and shouldn't do right now."

He bit my earlobe with a growl, then kissed away the sting. "I had a full physical a month ago. All my tests came back negative. Haven't been with anyone since." His lips continued down my jaw and I tilted my head back to give him better access. He was branding me with his lips and teeth and tongue and I knew I would feel him under my skin forever.

"I had every test under the sun after..." I refused to talk about another man right now. "Throat culture too. Negative. I'm on the Depo shot. I have condoms in my purse."

He breathed my name against my skin and I broke out in goose bumps. I needed to hear that when he was inside me. "Fuck. The thought of me in your mouth..."

I smiled, nipping at his collarbone. "I think that could be arranged." I sank to my knees, lifting up his shirt and kissing his stomach on the way down. A dusting of hair darkened as it dipped below his jeans. "Shirt off."

He complied, seams screaming in protest at his rough movement. My eyes widened at the amazingly sexy man in front of me. I momentarily forgot what I was doing and got lost in his gorgeous, broad shoulders, his muscles shaped and molded from manual labor.

My fingertips ran across a tattoo on his rib cage and my stomach clenched in recognition as I read the words. They were lyrics to a song from my favorite band, Sorry Charlie. A song I had sent to him via email after a losing battle with a bottle of wine. Really, alcohol and Luke were clearly a bad combination.

I wish I could fuse
My love to you
With one more goodbye kiss
I'm yours to miss
I hate being far away
But you know that I can't stay
So please let me fuse my heart to you

"Luke..." I looked at him, searching his face. It was my favorite line from my favorite song by my favorite band. What did it mean that it was tattooed on him? Also, it looked super cool and I wanted a matching one.

My heart thudded once, twice, three times. How had I never realized how I felt about him before, when I'd been sending him lyrics like that?

He leaned over and kissed me hard, rocking me back on my heels, and there was no more thinking. He kissed me as though he was afraid this moment would end if he stopped. My hands went to the soft leather of his belt and I yanked it apart, letting my hands trail down his zipper, which was badly bent out of shape.

When he finally released my mouth, I licked my lips in anticipation. Button undone, jeans pulled down, boxer briefs shoved aside. Finally, his hard length was in my hand. Heat pooled low in my abdomen and I knew my underwear was soaked. I was so ready for him.

But first, I needed to taste him. Starting with a soft kiss, then a lick, then a suck, I took him into my mouth, getting lost in learning the sounds he made and what made him jerk forward. I wanted to spend hours, days, weeks memorizing every inch of this man. He gripped the back of my head, thrusting between my lips. It was so damn hot, and I couldn't stop the low moan deep in my chest.

Too soon, he pulled away, panting. "Stop, stop. I'm about to explode and I want to be in you."

"You were in me," I teased with a smile, letting him help me up.

His mouth claimed mine while he tried to pull off my dress, which was counterproductive. My arms got tangled and I laughed, pulling away to try to escape. "God, it's like I'm eighteen again."

"Making up for prom night," Luke teased, freeing my arms and tossing my dress. His mouth followed the straps of my bra down my arms before he quickly released the clasp with one hand. He trailed his eyes over me and let out a rush of air. "Reeses, you're beautiful."

My insides turned to goo and I straightened my shoulders, my breasts pressing into his bare chest. Skin against skin. I didn't know how my fire alarms weren't going off because I was burning up. "Luke," I breathed, and kissed him again.

We stumbled toward the couch, neither of us bothering to look where we were going. He was on top of me, pulling off my underwear, when I heard Sergeant Cornflakes crow. I ignored my bird. Chances were he was crowing at the moon or something.

Luke's fingers grazed my seam and we both groaned. "You're so wet," he breathed. "I can't wait to—"

A manly shout cut off his sentence. Luke froze and covered me with his body, turning to face the intruder. I turned to stone, all of the heat and need turning to ice. I looked over Luke's shoulder to see my brother's back. "What happened?!"

"I'm so sorry! I'm so sorry!" Jami said. "I should've called. I used my key—oh God, just pretend I was never here."

"Jami, it's okay," Luke said, reaching for a blanket on the back of the couch and covering me.

"Jay, what's wrong?" I covered my front and let Luke help me to a sitting position. He quickly tucked himself back into his pants and zipped up. My entire body cried out in protest.

But I didn't have time to think about naked Luke when my big brother was standing in front of me, clearly distraught. He turned to face us with his hands over his eyes. Even hiding, I could see the tell-tale signs of tears. Puffy cheeks and red under his nose. My heart stuttered, and I wanted to run to him and hold him. But, shirt first.

Luke spoke first. "Jami, go into the kitchen. Edie will be right in."

"I should go. I'm so sorry." His voice broke and my heart hurt.

"No, stay. I'm going," Luke said.

"You're not going anywhere, Jami!" I ordered. "I'll be right there, I promise."

My brother nodded and turned toward the kitchen. I didn't miss the slump of his shoulders and his shaking hand. I turned to Luke and wrapped my arms around him. "I'm so sorry, I need to—"

He pressed a soft kiss to my lips, interrupting me. "Don't apologize. Go clean up. I'll make tea."

Goddamn heart. It was doing an interpretive dance of gratitude as I kissed Luke again before running upstairs. I dressed quickly and splashed water on my face, trying to calm any residual smolder.

Jami was cradling a mug when I made it back to the kitchen. Luke handed me a cup with two tea bags when I walked in, mint and chamomile. My favorites. He put an arm around my waist, kissing the side of my head. "I'll talk to you tomorrow, okay?"

I nodded. "Thanks."

With a soft kiss to my lips, he left. I took a sip of my perfect tea. If this man did not want me to be in love with him, he was doing it wrong.

Jami closed his eyes. "I'm so sorry, sissy. I didn't think."

"Don't apologize." I scooted my chair over and sat next to him, my shoulder against his. "Start at the beginning."

CHAPTER SEVENTEEN

EDIE'S TIP #18: MARK MY WORDS: THE CAR
COMPANY THAT DEVELOPS A CAR THAT CAN MAKE
COFFEE OR TEA WILL TAKE OVER THE WORLD.

JAMI GAVE ME A SIDEWAYS GLANCE. "Are we going to talk about what I walked in on?"

I narrowed my eyes. "Absolutely not."

"Eds—"

"We aren't talking about it! We're talking about why you're in my kitchen with red eyes at one in the morning." I playfully elbowed his ribs. "I thought you had a date."

He shifted uncomfortably in his chair and took a fortifying sip of tea. "We did. And he was perfect. It was me who messed up." He covered his face with his hands and shook his head. "I went to therapy. I moved across the country and started over, but it still—" He broke off and took an unsteady breath. "It still terrifies me."

I laid my head on his shoulder, gripping his bicep. "I know." Truthfully, it terrified me, too, and I hadn't been the one who lived it. But I'd never forget the phone call that night.

Jami's hands fell from his face and he cradled his mug. "He's so pretty. I'm stupid around him."

"I find it hard to believe you're stupid about anything."

He put his hand on top of mine. "I literally forget my name when he kisses me."

I let out a low whistle. "Hello, sailor."

He smiled, but it didn't reach his eyes. "We were having so much fun and then he pulled me around the back of this building and kissed me and it was..." He let out a whoosh of air. "It was the best kiss I've ever had. It's like I've been waiting for him my entire life."

I bit my lip, blinking away the images of the man who had just walked out the door. *No. Stop thinking about Luke. Focus.* "What happened?"

He shrugged. "Some asshole kids shouted 'fag' out the window of a car and I froze. I just shut down. How could I do this again? What if work finds out and it all happens again? How could I risk everything for a man I just met?"

I wrapped my arms around him and put my head on his back. "Honey, it's okay." We rocked back and forth for a few moments. "I don't know what you went through. I don't know what it's like to walk down the street and be worried I'm going to get the shit beat out of me for holding the hand of someone I love."

I pulled back and brushed his hair from his face. "But I do know what it's like to get that phone call in the middle of the night that my big brother is in the hospital after being beaten, and I know what it's like to be fucking terrified." I gripped the front of his shirt. "But you get this through your head right now—you can't let hate win. You have so much love to give and any man would be lucky to have you."

He rolled his eyes. "Thanks, Mom."

I flicked his nose. "Did you tell him?"

He frowned and shook his head. "No, I told him I wasn't ready to be 'out,' and he told me he was too old to be dating someone in the closet. And that was it."

"Well, shit." I got up and walked over to the fridge, pulling out an open bottle of wine. Grabbing two more mugs from the dish rack, I pulled the cork out with my teeth and sloshed a healthy portion in each. "Screw tea. We need alcohol."

Jami accepted the mug and took a long drink before putting his head down on his arm. "Tell me something good. Make tonight better."

I shrugged. "I mean, I saw Luke mostly naked, so that was a bonus."

My brother lifted his head and stared at me for a long moment before bursting out laughing. He ran a hand down his face and shook his head. "Oh God, that was not what I expected to find when I walked in."

I cringed. "I'd say I'm sorry, but I'm not."

Jami took another gulp of wine. "I wouldn't be if the man I'd been in love with since I was eight was mostly naked and on top of me."

I choked on my wine, my nasal passages burning in protest. I slapped Jami's arm as I mopped up my face with a napkin and blew my nose. "I hate you," I wheezed. "I was not in love with him at eight. I'm not even sure I liked him until a few weeks ago."

Jami rolled his eyes. "Lies. You've loved him since he got all of your Hot Wheels cars out of the trash when Mom threw them away. He smelled so, so bad after, but you didn't care. You just kept hugging him. I knew right then."

I stared at him, looked down at his mug, then back up at him. "No more wine for you."

He shrugged. "Not my fault it took you seventeen years to figure it out. Too bad you had to go through Will first. I mean, Will's hot, but he's like the worst mansplainer I know."

"Well, we now know crazy is an inherited gene. Because you're off your rocker."

His laugh filled the room and I breathed a sigh of relief. That laugh usually meant the worst was over. It had taken years for him to laugh like that after he moved home. "I love you because you're so oblivious with guys, and it's one of my favorite things about you."

I flipped him off, then finished my wine and stood up to rinse our mugs. "It was probably a good thing you came when you did. Two minutes later..."

Jami banged his head on the counter. "I would've been scarred for life."

I hit his arm with the kitchen towel I was drying my hands with. "Way to be my wingman."

He gave me his big brother look. "I know you're an adult and don't need me telling you what to do, but be careful. Luke isn't the sticking around type. And sleeping with him isn't going to save the shop."

My stomach clenched and I leaned against the kitchen counter, my eyes trained on the back door. "I know." I looked at Jami. "He has a tattoo of Sorry Charlie's 'Fuse' on his rib cage."

Jami stared at me for a long moment. "Well...fuck. What are you gonna do?"

I shrugged. "Buy a new vibrator and not shave my legs. Maybe wear a bodysuit that takes scissors to get off."

Jami stared at me with a look of pure horror and covered his ears. "LALALA I can't hear you!"

This time I threw the towel at him and it hit him in the face. He pulled it off and sighed. "Okay, but in all seriousness, you—"

"Nope." I grabbed the towel and draped it over the oven handle. "We're not talking about it. It will never be casual with him and casual is the only option. It was a mistake, never going to happen." I pointed my finger at him. "You, on the other hand, need to talk to your man."

He rubbed his forehead with the heel of his hand. "Yeah. Probably. Maybe give my therapist a call."

I nodded. "Good plan." I tilted my head to the side. "Come on, guest room."

When he stood, he pulled me into a really tight hug, resting his chin on the top of my head. "Thanks, sissy."

"Anytime, big bro."

On my way upstairs, I grabbed my clutch and fished out my phone. I refused to look at the screen until I was safely locked in my bedroom and had the top sheet pulled over my head.

Luke: Is Jami okay?

My heart thudded. He cared about my brother. Dammit!

Me: He's okay. We talked and made a game plan.

Luke: Good. I know I shouldn't say this, but I can't stop thinking about you.

I held the phone to my chest and closed my eyes, warmth radiating to the tips of my fingers and toes. I started typing. *I can't stop thinking about you in my mouth.* Deleted. *I can't wait to see you again.* Deleted. *Why do you have to be such a great guy?* Deleted.

I sat up, dislodging the sheet, and growled. I needed to stop this nonsense. I typed *Goodnight Luke* and hit send, then shut off my phone. Tonight was a fluke. It had to be.

CHAPTER EIGHTEEN

EDIE'S TIP #13: SOMETIMES UNEXPECTED TRAFFIC
JAMS LEAD TO THE BEST STORIES. OTHER TIMES
THEY LEAD TO A MOSQUITO BITE ON YOUR ASS
FROM PEEING IN THE WOODS.

BY THE TIME I rolled out of bed the next morning, Jami was already awake and making eggs and avocado toast. After some muttering about how disgusting gluten-free bread was—and really, for eight dollars a loaf it should taste better—I called Tina for our bi-monthly Skype date. She was so excited to see Jami and my pink hair, she couldn't sit still.

"Mom is going to destroy this child," Jami lamented after we hung up. "She's so awesome and Mom will passive aggressive it out of her."

I pursed my lips. "This is why I keep in contact with her. Maybe she'll see as she grows up that she can be herself with us."

Jami drank another cup of coffee before rubbing his face with both hands and groaning. "I guess it's time for me to stop making excuses. Time to go home, shower, and man up."

I bumped his shoulder with mine. "What's the worst thing that could happen? He's not interested? You'll still be in the same place you are right now."

He winced. "Just more hits to my pride."

"And if he is interested?"

He turned his head to me and leaned against the couch. "Then Mom is going to lose her shit when she finds out I'm gay. At least it might take some of the attention off you."

I mirrored his pose. "But that's not a position I want you in. She may love me, but she's never liked me. She adores you to the moon and back."

He shrugged. "That's because she sees me how she wants to. I'm her first-born son, destined for great things."

"I'm just the daughter who made all the wrong choices."

He reached over and grabbed my hand. "You had a better relationship with Grandpa than she did. Didn't you ever notice?"

I frowned. "He loved Mom."

He squeezed my hand. "He did. But she chased after his approval, and if you were in the room, you took all the attention. She's taking out her insecurities and resentment for him on you. You never needed her, but you both needed him."

I opened my mouth and closed it again. I didn't know what to say.

"You did nothing wrong, and she needs to go to therapy. Next time you're fighting, look at her. Really look at her. She's just a lost little girl."

"You sound just like Dad. How do you know all this?" I whispered.

He shrugged. "I'm older and I'm a lawyer. I can read body language." He kissed the top of my head, cleaned up our dishes, and left, leaving me wading through an ocean's worth of thoughts.

I absentmindedly started my Sunday chores as my mind raced through all of my interactions with Mom, her engagement to Will being the biggest neon sign. By the time I had Swiffered, vacuumed, cleaned my toilets, and started a load of laundry, my head was spinning.

If what Jami said was true, it explained why she had so much resentment for the shop. Once this house and shop were gone, she would feel she'd won against Grandpa, and in a way, against me.

122

But I wasn't going to give up my dreams for her ghosts. I needed to make a plan. I was New Edie, Stronger Edie, and the shop needed to reflect that.

My stomach grumbled, and I glanced at my watch. Okay, grocer and lunch, then plan. I threw on my sandals, then grabbed my purse and reusable grocery bags.

The moment I opened the door, I heard Sergeant Cornflakes's intruder alarm echo through the late morning. With a sigh, I closed and locked my front door and tossed the bags over my shoulder, hurrying down the path.

Most likely someone had busted their tire and needed help changing it. Working hours only mattered for my employees. If I was around, I would check out anyone's vehicle. It was my responsibility as a businesswoman in a small town.

My steps faltered when I saw the shiny black Audi in my parking lot. This wasn't a resident with a popped tire. This was the dragon.

I took a deep breath, trying to calm my instant flare of resentment and anger. I would reserve judgment until I figured out what game she was playing. I could be the bigger person. I could be the daughter I wanted to be even if she wasn't the mother I needed her to be.

Sergeant Cornflakes ran out of the propped-open front door, dropping feathers and crowing so loud they could probably hear it in the next town over. I crouched down. "Whoa, whoa, buddy. What's wrong?"

He ran in a circle around me and I scooped him up, petting his soft feathers. He was still making low clucks but was calmer. I let him go and he wandered off toward the opposite side of the street.

I guess now we knew why the chicken crossed the road—to get away from my mother.

Two steps into the shop and all my good intentions were gone.

My mother and Will were inside, speaking to a man in a golf shirt and khakis. All of my toolboxes and carts were mysteriously missing, along with Sergeant Cornflakes's bedding. "What the hell do you think you're doing?!" I shouted. "Get out of my shop!"

With a screech, the dragon ran at me, her heels slipping a little on the concrete. "Edith, I'm showing around our potential investor, David Spurs." She gestured to a man who was probably a few years older than her and so tan, his skin looked like leather.

I did not reach out and shake his hand but instead kept my focus firmly on my mother's pouty lips. "Where are my tools? Where are the chairs for the waiting room?" I looked at the blank walls. "Where's the artwork? Grandpa's calendar?"

Mom pressed her hands down in front of me. "I knew you'd react badly, which is why we weren't going to tell you. But Mr. Spurs is very interested in the condo idea and the market is hot, hot, hot!" She clapped with each "hot." "Now, don't be rude. Why don't you grab us a cup of..." She narrowed her eyes and took another step toward me, then froze. Her mouth fell open. "What the heck happened to your hair? Is this some kind of Kool-Aid rinse?"

She reached out to touch my ponytail, and I slapped her hand away. "Get out before I call the cops."

Mom turned to her guest with a smile. "Mr. Spurs, I apologize, but I need to have a word in private with my youngest child."

"Middle child," I muttered.

My mother ignored me. "Can you please give us a moment?"

He nodded and raised his cell phone. "Gotta make a few calls."

The moment he was gone, Will hurried over and put his arm around Mom's shoulders. "I own this property too. It's not trespassing." He pulled her into his side. "And since she's my business partner and my fiancée, I don't think the cops will even bother showing up." He eyed my hair and wrinkled his nose. "You're a little old for teenage rebellion, Edith."

I shoved my hand in my pocket and dug out my cell phone, hitting Luke's number. "Get to the shop immediately, or I'm going to be charged with homicide." I hung up without waiting for an answer. Either he'd show up and take care of the mess he'd help make, or I'd get twenty-five to life.

Mom pointed at me. "You go back home. Let the adults handle

this. When you're ready to grow up, you can be part of the shop discussion too."

When you're ready to grow up? I was the one who ran this business. I was the one who'd taken care of Grandma and Grandpa when they got sick. And I was done with her bullshit.

I sprinted to the fire extinguisher on the wall next to the office and snatched it from its cradle. I removed the pin and blasted her with a cloud of white.

My mother screamed, jumping back and shouting vague threats about suing me and calling the cops. Will tried to jump forward to tackle me, so I sprayed him too. Then I just kept blasting them both, spray after spray. This was so much fun! Why hadn't I thought of this before?

They made a beeline to the front door and stumbled into the parking lot. I locked the door and stayed inside until Luke took the turn into the parking lot so hard two of his tires almost left the ground. He jumped out of his truck, marched over, and stopped dead. I ran out to meet him, still shaking with rage.

He looked between the three of us—me with my fire extinguisher and the two ghosts by my side—and covered his mouth with his hand, but not before I saw his smile. "What—" He cleared his throat against a bubble of laughter. "What is going on here?"

Will and Mom were talking over each other. "We were trying to show our investor around!" "She ruined my designer clothes!" "I'm calling the police for assault!"

I leaned over to Luke. "Is it creepy I can't actually tell which one is saying what?"

Luke shook his head. "They're made for each other. I don't know why I didn't see it before."

Will, looking a little less like a drowned rat, pulled Mr. Spurs off to the side, no doubt to demean my character even more. Oh well. It was totally worth it.

Then my mother took aim and fired. "You are an embarrassment to this town, your family, and especially me! From the time you could talk, you have made my life miserable. I had to constantly fight with you to do your homework, to be a proper lady, to have manners. Now, you are parading around like a hussy with pink hair. I hope you'll have a modicum of respect for me and change it back before the wedding. You are the most selfish person I know."

I didn't think her words could still hurt me. But these sliced me open. No matter how lost a parent felt, or how much a child drifted away, no child wanted to hear they'd made their parent's life miserable.

Even though the hurt little girl inside of her was poking her hand out and waving frantically, it didn't make the words unsaid. It didn't make them hurt any less. I stumbled backward and dropped the fire extinguisher, completely deflated. But I was not going to let her see me cry.

Without a word, I walked back into my shop and locked the door behind me. I heard arguing, but didn't care. Flipping on my stereo, I loaded up my Sorry Charlie album and turned up the volume until it drowned out the loud voices outside. Grabbing the shop vac, I got to work cleaning up the fire extinguisher mess.

When I heard a key in the door, I didn't bother to turn around. I assumed my mother and Will were not dumb enough to try to enter the shop again, so it had to be Luke. He didn't say anything as he took a look around.

We were silent as we opened the door to the employee lounge to find the waiting room chairs and shop tools. He helped me move them back to their proper places, then helped me rehang the wall art and Grandpa's calendar. The art wasn't glamorous—a few water-colors my grandma had done, two drawings of the auto shop from local kids, and a portrait of Sergeant Cornflakes that Kristy had given me as a birthday present last year—but they were the special touches that made the shop feel like so much more than just a workspace.

When we were done, Luke walked over to me, wrapped me in his arms, and hauled me against him. My nose stung as the words my mother said rattled around in my head. I tried to pull away so I could find a bathroom to hide in, but Luke wouldn't let me.

He just put his hand to the back of my head and held me against his chest, swaying back and forth. I proceeded to hiccup-sob everywhere. Snot, tears, and all the anxiety and anger that had been building for weeks.

His whispered words of comfort, promises that my mother was wrong in every way, and gentle "shhh, shhh" washed over me as the sobbing slowed to just a steady stream of tears. I cried my heart out, only calming down when my favorite song came over the speakers

The one Luke had tattooed on his chest.

We swayed back and forth, my tears drying up while his low voice whispered the words against my hair.

I wish I could fuse
My love to you
With one more goodbye kiss
I'm yours to miss
I hate being far away
But you know that I can't stay
So please let me fuse my heart to you

My heart reached out and grabbed his, trying to keep it here, trying to keep him here. But I knew the moment I stepped away, I would lose hold of him. I wanted to tell him how I felt, wanted to beg him to stay, but today wasn't the day. I wasn't sure if any day was the day.

I should ask him to tell me more about Alice May. Ask him all the questions I was afraid to voice. But I didn't. Because I was more of a chicken than Sergeant Cornflakes.

He pulled back when the song ended and used his thumbs to caress my cheeks. I cringed when I saw the wet front of his shirt. "I'm sorry," I whispered, my voice gravelly.

"Doesn't matter," he said. "Come on, I'll walk you home."

He kept me close to his side as he let us out the front door and locked it behind him. As we walked up the path, my rooster waddled toward us, did a circle, then scurried back to his coop behind the house. I liked to think he was checking on me.

Once inside, Luke put me on the couch, took my shoes off, and lifted my legs so I was lying down. He grabbed a blanket and covered me, tucking me in like a burrito. Going into the kitchen, he made my favorite tea and set the cup on the coffee table.

He sat on the edge of the couch and brushed my hair out of my face. "Nap. If you feel like dinner later, I'll come over and cook. I've been looking up some gluten-free recipes."

My eyes welled up again and I bit my lip, trying to control my emotions. He was perfect...except for the leaving thing. "Stay," I whispered. I meant more than right now, more than today. I meant always.

He smiled sadly. "I would, Reeses, but I need to take care of something. Text me when you wake up." He took his time kissing me, making sure to remind me how much he cared about me. His lips moved delicately over mine, chaste and innocent, but my heart still raced and my toes still curled.

Maybe I needed to add in some cardio to my week. Could a heart explode from kissing? Who cares; what a way to go.

He touched my nose with his index finger. "Text me later."

I watched him walk away and out the door. My heart, which had been clinging to his so tightly, was left pouting when we were alone again.

CHAPTER NINETEEN

EDIE'S TIP #9: GOOD HEADLIGHTS ARE LIKE A
GOOD BRA: SUPPORTIVE AND STABILIZING WHEN
YOU'RE ON THE MOVE.

DESPITE LUKE'S ORDERS, I didn't nap. I drank my tea, ate a bowl of ice cream, washed my face, and jumped on the stationary bike in my basement. With ear-splitting music and sweat pouring off of me, I made a plan.

There was almost no way I was going to get the money to buy the shop from Luke in time, but I was going to go down fighting. When my legs were jelly, I took a quick shower and put my damp hair into a braid. Then I called Jami.

"Hey, sissy!" He sounded happy and my sharp mood dulled around the edges.

"You with Caden?"

I could practically hear his smile. "You were right. You can gloat later."

I laughed. "Excellent, I'll hold you to that." I took a deep breath. "I need your help."

"Shoot."

"How fast can you bake like three dozen cupcakes and a few loaves of zucchini bread?" While I'd inherited the car genes, Jami had our grandma's baking genes. It was his attention to detail and the way he could extrapolate data. He hadn't ventured into the gluten-free side yet, but I was convinced he would make my next birthday cake.

I heard a rustling as if he were moving the phone from one position to another. "Uh...depending on a lot of things, but with your double ovens, extra muffin pans, and nothing terribly fancy, a few hours? Why?"

"I'm going to have a bake sale. And maybe a car wash. Get your car washed and then get some baked goods! It's perfect."

He chuckled. "Okay, when?"

I bit my lip. "This Wednesday?"

There was a long pause. "Like in three days Wednesday?"

"Yes?" I said, but it came out like a question.

He sighed. "Yeah, okay. I'm calling Kristy too. She can help. And maybe Fran from the bakery will donate something."

I squealed. "You're the best!"

"Yeah, yeah. But I'm not washing cars. "

SHOP STAFF MEETINGS were typically on Sundays, although with usually more than an hour notice. Like my grandpa, I tried to avoid closing the shop early for any reason, with the exception of inclement weather. Even then, I had to be in the office as there were only two tow trucks in Grenadine. I took the day shift and a local bar owner, Earl, took the night shift for fun. Hey, whatever floated his boat...er, towed his truck?

When the crew met me in the employee lounge around three, they were antsy. Lots of whispering and side-eyes happening. "Should we be freaked?" Rosa asked, her eyes narrowing. "I can't tell. Her cheek isn't twitching."

Henry lifted his glasses off his face and gave me a quizzical look. "You look like you did when Chris Osgood retired from the Red Wings."

I pointed at him. "You know he was my Wing, Henry."

"Oh God, you're leaving with Luke and going to let him impregnate you for the next decade!" Jackie, my part-timer, cried.

Tamicka shrugged. "I mean, have you seen that man? Have you seen his *hands*?"

"The man does have nice hands, Edie," Henry added.

Oh dear Lord, this had to stop. I mean, not that I wouldn't let Luke impregnate me—NO, I was not going down that road today. I put my fingers in my mouth and whistled. "Yo, listen up!"

Everyone stared at me.

"We need to talk." I swallowed, my throat dry.

"I knew I should've gone to college," Rosa muttered before saying a few choice words in Spanish. "*Mi madre* is going to kill me if I lose this job."

I silenced her with a glare and then told them everything. Well, not *everything*, just about the shop. When I finished, there was total and complete silence. All of them were staring at me like I had grown a unicorn horn, changed into a leotard, and announced I was moving to the woods to "be one with nature." Ew. Nature.

Henry stood and walked over, pulling me into his arms. "Your grandpa would've rolled up that newspaper for not telling us this the day it happened!"

I held onto his forearms when he pulled away. "I know. I was so freaked, I didn't know what to do."

His mustache twitched. "Ed used to say, 'Sure, you can rebuild an entire car yourself. But it's easier with friends.'"

I sucked my lips into my mouth and nodded. He did say that, and I needed to listen.

Jackie had her hand up. "I'm willing to take a thirty percent pay cut for the next month if it means putting more money into the fund. I have some savings."

Chieka put her hand up. "Me too, Edie."

Rosa raised her hand. "I can't take a pay cut. The money helps *mi familia*. But I'll help with whatever you need outside of work—social media, fundraisers, anything you got."

I snapped my fingers and pointed at her. "We're going to host a bake sale and car wash on Wednesday. Bring me whatever food you can! Call everyone you know."

She nodded. "I'll get José and Diana to come help wash cars. I'll make some churros. White people love churros."

Tamicka nodded. "Girl, so do brown people."

"And tan people!" Chieka added.

Rosa laughed. "Okay, okay, *everyone* loves churros. I get it."

Henry nodded. "I'll get Delores to wrangle up something and I'll grab the equipment we need for a car wash. I have a Costco membership."

I would not cry. I would *not* cry.

"You guys," I sobbed, covering my face and bending over at the waist. They all tackled me in a group hug. We stayed locked together until Sergeant Cornflakes walked into the room, looked at us with his judgy, beady eyes, crowed, and waddled away.

We all cracked up and Rosa ran after him, taking pictures. "I'm making him his own social media account," she called. "He's going to rule the world one day!"

"Or my Crock-Pot!" I yelled back.

Rosa poked her head back into the room. "You wait and see, Edie." With a wink, she was gone.

I clapped and turned back to everyone. "Get out of here! Go enjoy the rest of your weekend. Remember, tell *everyone* about the carwash and bake sale. Wednesday! All day."

BY THE TIME four thirty rolled around, Tamicka had made a press release for the *Grenadine Herald* and posted the information all over social media. Rosa was rambling in a text about some event page she created and promised her siblings were in for sure. Delores had called me about recipes and then promptly called her sister to help.

I was so engrossed in scribbling down the plan in my notebook, I screamed when my phone chimed. Looking around to make sure no one saw me in my empty house—okay, maybe I was losing my mind—I unlocked the screen to see a text from Luke.

Luke: You awake and up for company?

I smiled.

Me: Yes please! Come over.

I stared with impatience at the three dots that announced he was typing. "Come on!" I told the phone. In reality, it was probably thirty seconds, but it seemed like an hour.

Luke: Be there in twenty.

Luke: To be clear, I'm not expecting anything more than to feed you dinner

I pursed my lips. Well, how did I feel about that? It was a really, really good idea to not do anything with Luke. But we were going to be alone in my house.

Me: Okay

Okay?! What the hell kind of response was that? How about *Can I kiss you again*—No. Stop.

Checking the time, I let out a little scream and ran upstairs. I needed to put on the right outfit—one that was cute but not trying too hard but not too casual. I settled on a scoop neck tank top, a bra other than a sports bra, and my favorite jeans.

After pulling my hair from its braid, I sprayed some of the fancy hairspray from Kristy onto the waves and threw on some mascara and Chapstick. I left my feet bare, but only because the doorbell rang as I was standing in front of my sock drawer.

Luke smiled so wide when he saw me, I forgot my middle name. "You look perfect," he said, stepping into the house and kissing my cheek. My knees wobbled. I stood there like an idiot for a few moments too long, before my brain caught up.

I grabbed the two paper bags from his hands and nodded to the kitchen. "Let's see what you can wrangle up."

Luke chuckled. "Edie, my entire family came from Italy. If I can't cook you a little pasta, *mia madre* will haunt me."

I laughed, setting his bags on the counter. "Well then, proceed."

Watching Luke cook was like a drug. He was confident, calm, and his brow always furrowed when he read over the recipe. I was addicted. Despite my offers to help, he brushed me off and set a glass of wine in front of me.

Fine by me; I was enjoying the view. He was wearing dark jeans and a soft light-green shirt that showcased his shoulders. The shirt made his eyes glow like lanterns, and those jeans...and his ass...I couldn't look away.

"How was the rest of your day?" he asked as he dumped a mound of vegetables in some sizzling oil.

"Good! I planned a bake sale and car wash."

Luke nodded. "Awesome. When?"

"Wednesday."

"I'm there." He opened up my spice cabinet and then looked at me. "This was not what I expected."

I laughed as he reached into the perfectly organized cupboard. "That was all Jami. He said my haphazard selection of store brand spices was shameful and promptly replaced and reorganized everything for my birthday." I shrugged. "I don't cook much."

Will, like Luke, had been a great cook. Something clearly inherited from their mother. It had been a steady diet of Ray's and brinner —breakfast for dinner—since I went gluten-free a year and a half ago. Will had no desire to change his recipes or cook two separate meals, so he just made whatever he wanted and left me to my scrambled eggs. In hindsight, that probably was another red flag.

Luke selected a plethora of spices and started putting them on things. He had a pot of boiling water and another one of amazing smelling sauce. Special gluten-free bread was warming in the oven and my mouth watered in anticipation. I had reviewed the label to make sure, but there was no need to worry. Luke was on top of it.

I was trying very, very hard to ignore the way my skin heated. It was totally just the oven. "What'd you do today?"

He looked back over at me before turning back to the stove.

"Went and saw Dad. Made some calls. Thinking about staying another week. Help get some of Dad's stuff organized, things like that."

My eyes widened. "Really? What about work? What about the money?"

The spatula hit the pan so hard, it rocked it. "It's all a maybe right now." He shrugged. "Playing it by ear."

We were both silent as he tasted the sauce and then shut off the burners. He began plating the food when the timer rang. The moment he opened the oven door, the warm, toasty scent of garlic filled the air. I groaned out loud. The baking sheet clattered on the counter.

"Everything okay?" I asked.

Luke nodded. "Yep, just..." He looked over at me. "Never mind. Let's eat."

When he'd finished prepping everything, he brought the plates to the bar and set them down. A beautiful rainbow of vegetables mixed with zucchini noodles, grilled chicken, and a splash of tomato sauce stared back at me. He had laid two pieces of the garlic bread across the top with freshly grated parmesan.

I almost fell off my stool. "Wow," I whispered, reverently.

"Eat up."

My eyes were wide as I looked between him and the most gourmet meal I had eaten since my doctor told me to go gluten-free. "Thank you," I whispered, hoping to express everything in those two words.

He laughed. "You haven't tasted it yet. It could be awful."

I shook my head. "No one but Ray has cooked me dinner since I stopped eating gluten. It's just...it's nice." Most gluten-free food was disgusting or full of sugar and was three times as expensive. I had cried after many a grocery store trip.

But Luke just walked in and made me dinner like it didn't faze him. My poor little heart couldn't take it. It tried to crawl out of my chest to hug him.

He booped my nose. "Well then, you're welcome. Eat."

The moment the taste explosion hit my mouth, I knew if I wasn't in love with Luke before, I was most definitely in love with him now. "Oh gawd," I moaned around the mouthful. "Itssogood!" The sauce was sweet but sharp, the chicken juicy and crisp, the noodles al dente.

Luke stared at me as I licked the sauce off my lips. His eyes darkened to Fathom Green, and my stomach flipped. If this food wasn't so damn good, I would've shoved our plates to the floor and climbed him.

But first, food.

I couldn't talk. I couldn't do more than moan and groan and make appreciative noises as I practically licked my plate clean. When I had finished shoving every last drop of sauce and crumb into my mouth, I sat back with my hands over my stomach. "That was...heaven."

Luke smiled his little boy smile. "Yeah?"

I knocked his knee with mine. "Yeah." He stood up and started gathering dishes. I grabbed his arm. "Nope! You cooked, I clean. It's the rules."

He scoffed. "I'm not going to make you clean when I offered to make you dinner."

I poked his chest. "I know you've been gone for a few years, but I'm sure, SURE you wouldn't cross my grandma's rules in her own house."

He grimaced. "Gah, the grandma card. Not cool, Becker. Not cool."

I laughed. "Go pick out a Wii game, Moretti. I want to kick your ass."

"You still have a working Wii?"

I shrugged. "How else would Jami and I have our annual Wii Tournament of Doom without one?"

"I'm not really sure why I ask questions. The answers are never what I expect them to be."

"Ah-ha! That's why."

He lifted his hands in a "what are you gonna do" gesture and walked into the living room. As soon as he was gone, I pulled my phone out of my pocket and texted Kristy.

Me: Help! I want to suck his face.

I distracted myself with putting away the food until she replied.

Kristy: I think u should go 4 it

Me: But he's my business partner. He's leaving. HE'S WILL'S BROTHER!

Kristy: He's the guy uv been in <3 with since you were 8

I rolled my eyes.

Me: I have not!

Kristy: Just bc it took u 17 yrs to figure it out doesn't mean the rest of us didn't catch on

Kristy: Stop txting me & go get some xxx

Me: Whatever

With a huff, I locked my phone and shoved it in my pocket and started scrubbing the pots and loading the dishwasher. The rhythm and routine had calmed me by the time I wiped down the sink. Grabbing two hard ciders and a package of Edie-safe cookies, I walked into the living room to find Luke flipping through the basket of games.

I handed him a cider and he held up Mario Kart. "I mean, is it really worth having any other game when we know this is the only game worth playing?"

"Yeah, 'cause I have to give you the chance to win at something." I shrugged. "We all know Mario Kart is mine. Want to pick another game?"

He raised his eyebrow. "Oh. It's on, Becker."

I took a long sip from my cider and took a deep breath. "Bring it, Moretti."

CHAPTER TWENTY

"NO! NO! NO!" Luke shouted, jumping off the couch and trying to use his whole body to steer.

Novice move.

The trick was to be calm and relaxed with your controller at all times. It was a baby and you were rocking it to sleep. And I was the controller master.

As Princess Daisy rode over the finish line in first place for the third time, Luke fell to his knees and lifted his controller in the air. "A PLAGUE ON BOTH YOUR HOUSES!" he yelled.

I cracked up and fell back against the couch. "I love that you just quoted Mercutio."

With a smile that made that damn bat in my chest flutter again, he sat down next to me, his hand resting on my knee. "The only redeemable character in that damn play, besides Benvolio. I like to imagine Mercutio faked his death and they ran off together."

I blinked, then blinked again. "For the dude who got a C minus in Mr. Baker's English class, you sure have strong opinions on Shakespeare."

"You made me watch that movie like fifteen times in one month."

I smacked his arm. "It was for a paper!"

"A two-page paper. You milked it. I was the only one crazy enough to watch it with you."

I shrugged. "Whatever. It's a badass movie."

He laughed, shaking his head and lifting up his controller. "One more?"

With a wink, I nodded. "One more." This time, I purposely drove off the course and took wrong turns. It was fairly obvious I was letting him win—and even then he was still having trouble—but when he came in second and I came in sixth, the smile on his face was worth it.

He set the remote down and turned on me. "You little cheater! You let me win!" Taking the controller out of my hand, he set it on the table before launching his tickle attack.

I should've seen it coming.

I attempted to slip off the couch and out of his reach, but he pinned my hands above my head and redoubled his efforts. I kicked the back of his knees, hard.

"Ow!" he said, releasing me and sitting up.

I gasped and sat up. "I'm sorry, are you okay?"

When he started laughing, I picked up a throw pillow and hit him across the face. He grabbed the pillow and tossed it off the couch, then leaned back in toward me. I scooted forward, pretending to lock him in a headlock.

He looked over at me, his gaze moving from my mouth to my eyes. My heart stuttered. "You're beautiful when you laugh."

All the breath rushed out of my lungs. "Luke..." I whispered.

He leaned on his elbow, bringing his face closer to mine. After brushing a piece of loose hair behind my ear, he gently pulled my head forward until our lips were inches apart. "I've never wanted anything more than to kiss you and keep kissing you."

I lifted an eyebrow. "Not even for real beating me at Mario Kart?"

His lips quirked. "Not even that." The inches between us became a centimeter, filled with our mingled breath. He didn't get closer, but instead waited for me to make up my mind.

"What happens when you leave?" I asked, searching his eyes.

A flicker of pain flashed across them and I winced. "My life is in North Carolina," he whispered. "I have to help take care of my friend and her new baby. It's why I need the money."

"Oh." That was all I managed to say. My chest tightened. Even though he was single, he wasn't free. Another woman needed his time and attention. I swallowed hard and smiled stiffly. "You're an amazing person, Lucas Moretti."

His nose bumped mine. "I wish you were able to come with me."

"Me too." I couldn't leave the shop and my girls. They were my squad, my found family. Anyway, he was going to be wrapped up in his own makeshift family. Grenadine was where I belonged. I just wished Luke and I belonged together, too.

He let out a long breath through his nose. "Maybe I should go."

What would I regret more? Doing something or always wishing I had? It was time to stop wishing.

I removed the distance between us and pressed my lips to his.

Luke's arms wrapped around me tightly, holding me in place. His kisses were sweet and slow, savoring me. His fingers trailed down my jawline and neck, tracing my collarbone, causing a riot of butterflies to flutter underneath my skin. The heat of his body crashed into me and I wrapped my arms around him, squeezing him tight.

I wanted more. I needed more. As he pulled back to end our kiss, I nipped at his bottom lip. He growled in the back of his throat and kissed me so hard my lips felt bruised.

Heat curled over every inch of my skin and I swear if I looked down, I'd be glowing. I wanted to luxuriate in him for hours, days, weeks. He needed to be naked; I needed to feel his velvet skin against mine *everywhere*. "Upstairs. Before someone interrupts us."

He trailed kisses down my neck and I tilted my head back to give him better access. The slide of his smooth lips and rough stubble shot sparks straight to my stomach, the smolder breaking into a flame. "Upstairs," he agreed against my skin. I shivered.

He wrapped my legs around his waist and hoisted me off the couch. His mouth was glued to mine as we climbed the stairs excruciatingly slowly. Sure, it would've been faster to stop sucking face long enough to get up the stairs, but where was the fun in that?

I pointed to my room and we walked in, Luke kicking the door shut behind him, and I locked it. He flipped on my desk lamp, then pulled my computer chair away from my desk, wedging it under the door handle. "No interruptions."

My stomach flipped. I was about to make love to *Luke*. It was surreal. When had this childhood friendship turned into something more? Why did he feel more right than Will ever had? I kissed him again, trying to clear my head of all the things I could worry about tomorrow.

If this was going to be the only night I had him, I wanted to remember it for the rest of my life.

He walked over to the bed and laid me down before covering me with his body. For the last two weeks, and maybe for the last several years, life had been spinning out of control. Grandma getting sick, then Grandpa and Mario. The diet change, the engagement, the breakup, and now the shop. But as soon as his weight settled on me, everything stopped. It was just him and me. The outside world, the worries, the shop, everything disappeared.

Stay.

He took my mouth again and I arched into him, my thigh rubbing against the amazing hardness trapped between us. I melted into the bed and through the floor. He pulled back, his nose bumping mine as he searched my face. "I never thought..." He kissed me so softly that my throat tightened with emotions I didn't want to think about. "I never thought I'd be this lucky."

"You didn't?" I whispered. A rush of heat covered my neck and face and I knew I was probably red. I didn't care.

"I've been crazy about you for a long time, Reeses."

Wait. Wait, what?! "Come again?" My eyes went so huge, they began to sting.

He smiled shyly and pulled back, shrugging one shoulder. "Do you think I would've dug your Hot Wheels out of the trash if I didn't think you were the coolest kid on the block? And then when I came home and saw you in that prom dress..." He shook his head. "You went from being that cool kid who always hung around to being a beautiful woman. Pretty sure I fell in love with you that night."

"I...love?" *Holy shit.* My skin burned and I'm pretty sure all of me was bright red. *Pretty sure I fell in love with you that night.* I couldn't breathe. What was breathing?

"Breathe." He chuckled, and kissed the tip of my nose. "Just always thought you were meant for..." *my brother.* The words rang clear, even though they were silent. "Someone else," he rushed.

My stomach pitched and a thousand questions bottlenecked in my mouth. What did this mean? Did it change anything? What happens tomorrow? What about next week?

Stay.

My heart was racing, and I just couldn't think about everything with his erection pressing against me. So I chickened out and put my hands on either side of his face. "Tonight, I'm yours," I whispered.

His top lip bumped mine, tilting my mouth upward. He carefully pressed his mouth to mine with a searing kiss, branding me forever. Embers fell from his lips into my haystack of a heart and it burst into flames, warming me from the inside.

Every inch of my skin begged to be touched as he deepened the kiss. My muscles tightened, my breath quickened, and need filled my veins. My heart thumped a hard warning, one last SOS, but the rest of my body told my heart to shut up.

This was Luke. *Luke.* He deserved to be savored.

Each kiss, each caress was harder, more desperate. I rolled us over and hit his head with mine. I sucked in a quick breath and pressed my hand to my forehead, but it was more shock than pain. He tried to rise up, but I shoved him down.

"I'm perfectly fine. Take off your shirt."

"I need that embroidered on something." Laughing, he balled the shirt up at the back of his neck and yanked it off so fast the seams strained. "Better?" His eyes were dancing in the yellow glow of my room.

I nodded because...what were words?

"You've got a bit of drool..." He reached up and thumbed the corner of my lips. I smacked his hand away and straddled him, his erection meeting the spot where I needed it most. His groan almost undid me.

He sat up and kissed me hard, our tongues tangling. I don't know who took my bra off, but I cried out when his mouth broke away from mine to lick and nip and suck down to my breast. I was drowning in his attention, that invisible thread inside me winding tighter and tighter. My fingers dug into his hair and I held tight as he brought me to the edge while I still had my pants on. "Luke," I groaned. "More."

He pulled back, his eyes nearly Tuxedo Black with desire. "Pants off."

He didn't need to ask me twice. I yanked off my jeans and underwear, almost falling off the bed in the process. I was graceful like that.

He struggled with his belt, but I came to his rescue, because I'm a giver. After discarding his clothes, I stared at him for a long moment, my entire body pulsing with the idea that his beautiful, hard length was about to be inside of me.

Luke.

Him.

I leaned over to my nightstand and pulled out a condom, then crawled up the bed. I paused to kiss the head of his erection, but he hissed and pulled back. "If you touch me right now, I'll make a mess."

I smiled. "Isn't that the point?"

He pinched my butt and my entire body throbbed. "I'm not twenty-one anymore. I need more than three seconds to reboot."

I immediately scrambled away with a salacious grin. "No touchy, got it."

He ripped open the condom and I watched, mesmerized, as he pinched the tip, then rolled it down his length. "Now, come sit on my face before I slide inside you."

I moaned at the words, my body desperate for his touch. As I crawled over him, embarrassment gripped me. I looked over at the light, wondering if it was too late to turn it off.

"Reeses," he whispered. "Look at me." My eyes found his. "You're perfect. And I need to taste you, or I think I'm going to die, right here. So please bring that amazing body to my mouth."

My insides twisted tighter and tighter at his words, and on shaking arms, I moved my hips over his face. Biting my lip, I closed my eyes, trying not to be self-conscious.

He kissed one thigh and then the other, whispering words that sounded like "beautiful" and "need" and "perfect."

He gripped my hips. "You're mine," he whispered into me, then kissed me softly. I sucked in a sharp breath as his lips moved over me like a first kiss.

He swirled and then he sucked, and I was floating off the bed and into the clouds. Nothing had ever felt like this before. I fisted the sheets as his tongue thrust inside me before finding my sensitive nub. He took his time exploring me with shallow kisses, then deeper kisses, and I moaned louder and louder.

My hips jerked as his rhythm increased and I grabbed onto the headboard, afraid I'd float away. "Luke, Luke, Luke," I repeated as he tightened his grip. His kisses became wild and relentless and I ground down onto his mouth. "Oh God, oh God," I groaned, my breath hitching as the sharp wave of energy hovered just out of reach. "I'm so close, so close."

He hummed against me and it pushed me over the edge, tumbling headfirst into an ocean of sensation. Wave after wave crashed over me as he took his time, lapping me up, tasting my pleasure. Every part of me was on fire. My nipples were so hard, they were almost painful. My legs shook and my arms turned to jelly.

I gasped for air as I descended from the clouds.

He held me in place until life returned to my useless limbs. Carefully, he helped me move down the bed and turned me onto my side, facing him. "Thank you," I whispered. I didn't need to tell him it'd never been like that, not with anyone. I knew he could see it in my eyes, could feel it in the way he kissed me when I tasted myself on his tongue.

His erection found my soaked wet folds. "Are you sure this is what you want?" he whispered.

"More than anything I've ever wanted in my life," I admitted, searching his eyes. "You?"

"Longer than you'll ever know." He kissed me slowly, lifting my leg over his thigh before running his hand over the smooth skin. "Why'd you stop sending the emails?"

I ran my fingers down his cheek and along his jaw. I had stopped sending them because Will had kissed me for the first time. Emailing Luke had been something so special and so emotional that it felt like cheating. My subconscious knew even then that my feelings for Luke weren't casual or platonic, even if the rest of me didn't. "I didn't think you still read them. You never answered me back."

His lips touched mine and he spoke against my mouth. "It was too hard. You made me homesick for *you*."

I breathed his name and he placed himself at my entrance. We were silent, still, savoring. A perfect moment suspended in time. We both sucked in one large breath and he pushed in.

I thought I would die. My heart raced as he filled me slowly, slowly, slowly. I moaned at the feel of him. So full. So *right*. It was like my body had been waiting for him my whole life. "Luke," I gasped.

He moved, making me arch against him. His arms pulled me tight against him. He was so deep, and I wanted to fuse our bodies together like this forever. I didn't care how awkward it would be to explain.

"I was right," he said against my lips. "You feel like home." He thrust hard, igniting the fire inside me again. He set a steady rhythm, and I was helpless in his arms. He kissed me everywhere he could, across my shoulders, along my collarbone, every inch of my neck.

All of my feelings poured out of me on my shaky breaths and whispers of his name, wrapping around us. Every inch of his skin pressed against mine and I tried to memorize every stroke he made. *Please remember this forever.* The fire inside grew hotter and hotter until the flames threatened to burn my skin away.

"So close, so close," I begged.

"Edith," he said through clenched teeth. "You're so amazing. Please baby, I need you to come."

His words caused a detonation.

Every muscle in my body tensed as pleasure rolled through me a second time. This time it was deeper, longer, on the knife-edge of pain as every muscle in my body wrung itself out. He made the sexiest noise I had ever heard low in his chest, and then he was throbbing inside of me, extending my orgasm. Tears filled my eyes as the pleasure overwhelmed me. The feelings. The love.

His lips kissed away the stray tear that escaped from my eye. We were both panting and sweaty, but it didn't matter. We searched each other's eyes, reading all the unsaid words and unshed emotions.

A small smile touched his lips as he brushed my hair out of my face. "I wish we had done this years ago."

I kissed him lightly. "Me too."

"You've ruined me for everyone else, you know."

I shrugged. "I'm not mad."

With one last kiss, he pushed himself up and went to the bathroom to clean up. He brought me back a cool washcloth and pressed it between my legs carefully. My cheeks heated with his ministrations, but then I remembered this was Luke. The most thoughtful guy I knew.

With one more kiss, I made my way to the bathroom, bouncing on the balls of my feet. I was alive, truly alive, for the second time in my life—the first time was after I'd changed my first transmission at eleven. Luke was waiting for me in my bed. Luke!

I cleaned up, washed my face, rinsed with mouthwash, and all but ran back to the bed. Luke opened his arms as I approached and I gladly slipped in next to him. He guided my head to his shoulder and ran his fingers through my hair and down my arm. Goose bumps followed everywhere he touched.

"You still staying at a motel?" I asked.

He nodded. "The one off seventy-five."

I lifted myself up on an elbow. "Why don't you come stay with me?"

"There are so many reasons I should say no to that." He tugged me back down.

"Like what?"

"Your mother. My brother."

I winced. "Accurate."

"But I will, if you want me. Because I don't want to stay away."

"I want you. Always." I flinched at the look on his face, knowing I'd taken it a step too far.

"Reeses," he said quietly. "I'm still leaving soon."

I tried not to tense, but when we were lying together, naked, it was kind of hard to hide. I cleared the ball of emotion from my throat. "I know," I lied. I was hoping I could change his mind. But if changing a person with sex was possible, then I had yet to see an example.

He kissed my forehead and took a deep breath. "I think it's time I told you the whole story."

CHAPTER TWENTY-ONE

EDIE'S TIP #3: SOME CARS YOU'LL REMEMBER FOR A LIFETIME. SOMETIMES BECAUSE IT'S AN AGERA RS, OTHER TIMES BECAUSE THERE ARE SNAKES LIVING IN YOUR DODGE SHADOW'S AIR VENTS.

MY HEART WAS in my throat as he began, knowing whatever ghosts he was about to reveal would be my mortal enemies. I considered getting dressed for this, but I didn't want to give him any reason to stop talking.

"When I was in the service, I lived off base. My neighbor was a really cool dude named Alberto." He shrugged one shoulder. "When I retired and went into disaster relief, I just stayed in that house. I liked North Carolina for the most part."

I ran my fingers over his collarbone, trying to give him silent comfort.

"We got really close. I even stood in his wedding."

My stomach twisted. I knew this story didn't have a happy ending because I knew Luke. I had only seen him cry a handful of times—at his mom's funeral, at both my grandparents' funerals—but his eyes were glistening now with memories.

"Six months ago, the mudslides in California hit. His cousins lost their home."

I kissed his shoulder, but I knew he wasn't even aware I was there anymore.

"He volunteered to come with me on the mission. Wanted to help any way he could, you know? What I didn't know at the time was if you volunteer with my disaster relief company, you're not covered by their life insurance. I never thought to ask."

My lips kissed his jawline and cheeks as he struggled to take a deep breath.

"We found a little girl alive in a house filled with mud. Walls collapsing down around her. There's no reason she should've made it. It was like there was this force field around her. We went in after her and everything came down."

He blew out a breath. "I got her out, went back in for him but—" He didn't turn away from me as a tear slipped down his cheek. "He was alive for twenty-three hours, long enough for his wife, Alice May, to say goodbye. I promised him I'd take care of her." He let out a shuddering breath. "She was two months pregnant."

Realization washed over me, and I knew with certainty that these few weeks were going to be the last we had. Luke was a man of his word. If he'd promised to take care of Alice May and her baby, he was going to do it, just like he took care of his mom when she'd gotten sick.

Images of the beautiful woman on his phone flooded my mind. He'd be there for her when she was overwhelmed, when she needed groceries, when she was too tired to feed the baby. He'd cut her lawn and repair her car. He'd be there for her in the same way he'd been here for me.

He'd make it his responsibility to be a second dad to the baby, to fill the void Alberto's death left behind. It was so Luke. He'd give up his life to make someone else's life easier.

And he couldn't do that in Grenadine.

He may come back to visit, maybe we'd even go out to dinner and talk about what was going on in our lives. I'd send him an email on his birthday and he'd never answer, like always. I fought to take a steadying breath. I could cry later, when he was asleep.

"They had just bought a house. She's in school to be a nurse."

I squeezed him tighter.

"When the hospital bills came in, she couldn't make her mortgage. I sold my place and moved in. We barely kept the power on. Now she's due in four weeks and there will be even more bills."

He covered his eyes with his arm, and I knew he was really crying now. "It's my fault." His voice cracked on the last word and my heart broke.

"*Shhh. Shhh.*" I pulled him as tightly as I could against me. "Have you seen a therapist?"

"I've had a few sessions with my old one while I've been home. She says it's not my fault."

"Do you believe her?"

He shrugged. "Logically."

I kissed the underside of his jaw. "So this vacation was just to get money?"

He shrugged. "Alice May's sister came into town to stay with her. They only have two bedrooms. Figured it was a good time to come out and get the shop situated, and I have tons of vacation stacked up at work."

Every muscle in my body tightened. Why did it have to come down to her or me?

Luke sniffled and shook his head. "Fuck, Reeses, I'm sorry." He moved his arm and wiped his face with the bedsheet. "I make love to you and then cry everywhere."

I rolled my eyes dramatically. "Ohmygosh, you were vulnerable in front of another human. Are you going to self-destruct?"

"It's very likely. You better come here and kiss me, just in case."

I pretended to think about it for a moment before I leaned over and kissed him hard.

LUKE SHOVED me up against the front door and kissed me until my toes curled. "I had you twenty minutes ago, and I need you again," he growled.

I laughed and gently slapped his arm. "Luke, I have to go open the shop and get you your money. But come on. Move in while you're here. Stop wasting money on the hotel."

He kissed me one more time and slowly stepped away. "I shouldn't. Especially once the gossip starts. But you're right, I can't afford to keep staying at the hotel."

"I'm always right."

He raised an eyebrow. "Uh-huh. Remember that time you handed me a glue stick instead of Chapstick?"

I rolled my eyes. "You really should look at things before you put them on your face. Anyway, come by whenever. Back door's open."

He smirked and stepped into my space again. "Oh, really?"

I laughed and kissed him. "Go!"

"I want to spend every moment with you that I can. Preferably naked."

I giggled. "Deal."

We strolled to his truck in the driveway and I kissed him one more time before he climbed in. My heart was swelling, even as he was pulling away. For this one moment in time, this would be our bubble of happiness. I'd deal with the fallout later.

When I spun on my heel to walk back into the house, I heard the unmistakable footsteps of the dragon. Her ears practically had smoke coming out of them. "Edith Doreen! How could you do such a thing to me?"

I blinked, taking a step back. *What the hell?* "What are we blaming me for today?"

She pointed in the direction Luke's truck went. "That is my fiancé's brother! Do you know what the people in this town will think if my *own daughter* is sleeping with her new uncle?!"

Oh, for fuck's sake. I patted my pockets for my phone and realized I had left it on the table along with my portable coffee mug. This was not going to be my morning. I turned my back to my mother and started up the porch steps. Her talons wrapped around my wrist and yanked me back down. I missed the last step and tweaked my ankle.

"WHAT THE HELL IS YOUR PROBLEM?!" I screamed, so tired. Tired of her drama, of her playing the victim. "The town doesn't care what I'm doing with Luke! And even if they do, he'll be gone soon anyway. You're the one who's getting married to YOUR DAUGHTER'S ex-fiancé. And quite frankly, I don't fucking give a shit what the town thinks."

She crossed her arms, shaking her head in apparent disbelief. "This is just like you. You can't be happy for me for one damn moment, can you?" She smacked her hand against her chest to emphasize her words. Her giant engagement ring glinted in the sun. That was my mother, always posing.

I turned around again, making sure my arms were tight to my front so she couldn't latch on. "Whatever you think, Mother, because clearly I'm always wrong." I started up the stairs.

"This last year with William has been the happiest year of my life and you don't even care!"

It wasn't her hysterical tone that stopped me this time. It was her words. Slowly, I turned half my body to face her, tilting my head. "I'm sorry, what did you say?"

She looked startled. "William makes me happy?" she said.

"No, what did you say, word for word."

She huffed, her hysteria changing to incredulity. "I don't see what this has to do with—"

"You said the last *year* with William has been the happiest year of your life."

If her forehead wasn't full of Botox, I knew she'd be frowning. "Yes, we started dating last August. I don't understand what—"

Her words went muffled as if we were suddenly at the bottom of a lake. Someone replaced my blood with ice water. I weaved on my feet and gripped the railing.

Will had been sleeping with my mother before we broke up.

Before we booked the venue and tasted the cakes. Before I bought the expensive dress I still needed to pick up from the shop and donate. I opened my mouth, but nothing came out.

"Edith, what is your problem?" She took a step forward, but I held out my hand. Whatever she saw on my face made her stop.

"Will and I didn't break up until after Thanksgiving," I whispered. "You were sleeping with my fiancé while we...while we..." I couldn't finish the sentence. Bile rose in the back of my throat. I had never been more thankful that I had stopped sleeping with Will long before our breakup.

My mother put her hand on her hip. "You're being a bit dramatic, don't you think?"

"Leave." My voice was loud, echoing in the still morning.

She reared back. "Excuse me?"

"Leave before I call the police for trespassing." I looked directly at the woman who'd given birth to me but hadn't been a real mother to me in years, if ever. "If you ever step foot on my property again, I will press charges. I don't want to see you, I don't want to talk to you, I don't want to hear your name. I'm not coming to your wedding, I'm not coming to Thanksgiving, Christmas, or your birthday. Are we clear?"

"Edith—"

"I am not joking. I will call the cops right now, I swear on my auto shop."

Her mouth fell open in disbelief. "You can't be serious."

"Show up without an invitation directly from me, and I swear to God I will tell all of social media what the two of you did to me behind my back."

"No, you wouldn't."

I lifted an eyebrow. "Do you really want to take that chance?"

She took a step back. "When you calm down, we'll talk about this."

"No." I shook my head. "We won't. If you have any messages for me, call Jami. Otherwise, I don't want to hear from you. And if you try, I will make that post."

Her mouth opened and closed, and she spun on her heel, walking away indignantly. I managed to make it through my front door before kneeling in my foyer and crying. Crying for the mother I had, crying for the one I didn't have. Crying for Will's betrayal. Crying for my own idiocy. I should've seen the signs. I should've known.

Then suddenly it was like my grandpa was standing next to me. I could hear his voice so clearly, I stopped crying. Hell, I stopped breathing.

When you're driving down the road to your dreams, you're going to hit potholes, get a flat, and maybe have an accident or two. A few people will even cause those accidents on purpose. But Edie, my girl, you know how we make a car drive again? By fixing one part at a time. Next time you're stranded, pull out your toolbox. Everything you need to get going again is right there.

I took a settling breath, the ache of missing him so strong I was drowning. I would give anything to hear his voice again. Anything to make him laugh. Anything to hug him.

But what I wouldn't do was stay here on the floor for one more second. I needed to get my ass to the shop and pull out that toolbox. I would have a lifetime to get over the Will-Mom thing. I only had a few more days to save the shop.

CHAPTER TWENTY-TWO

EDIE'S TIP #17: SURE, IT'S ABOUT WHAT'S UNDER
THE HOOD, BUT IT'S DEFINITELY ALSO ABOUT THE
SIZE OF THE BACK SEAT...

THE CAR WASH/BAKE sale was absolutely amazing and exhaust-
ing. After a quick call to Luke to summarize my mother's visit and his
appropriately expletive-filled response, I didn't even have time to
think about the Mom-Will situation. Instead, I spent the day taking
out my anger on mud splatters and cupcakes. Luke worked next to
me in a tight, white, wet shirt. It should've been illegal for him to look
that good. No wonder we got so many tips.

When Thursday morning rolled around, we were all zombies.
Jackie asked Rosa to cover her shift and Chieka texted she was
running late. Early August in Michigan could go from cool and rainy
to brutal and humid. We had obviously chosen to wash cars on a
ninety-five-degree day with ninety percent humidity. My nose was
red, my shoulders were pink, and my headache declared I should've
drunk more water.

My arms still ached from washing so many cars. My thighs
burned because I couldn't keep my hands off Luke after seeing him in
the wet shirt. Truly, I couldn't be blamed.

It took me two tries to make the coffee—it really helped to put
actual coffee in the machine—and I nearly stepped on Sergeant

Cornflakes when he ran by out of nowhere. I swear he was half cat. Tamicka flicked her hand in the air when she came in, but went directly to the office without bothering to say any actual words. I was anxious to find out the total amount we raised.

My eyes were only half opened when I flipped on the Open sign and unlocked the front door. Chieka shuffled in with her dark hair in a messy knot and her shirt hanging off her shoulder. "Incoming," she mumbled before disappearing into the office.

I was shocked to see Amy LeMarks, one of my mother's best friends, march in. To my knowledge, Amy had never once been in my shop. "Good morning, Mrs. LeMarks. What can I do for you?" My pulse quickened; I didn't like the look in her eyes.

She tucked her blonde bob behind her ear with a perfectly mani-cured nail and put her hand on her hip. "It's incredibly unprofes-sional to make your customers wait like that. If your shop is supposed to be open, it should be open!"

I glanced at my wall clock and then back at her. It was less than two minutes past. This woman was nuts. My customer service mask slid on. "I apologize for my tardiness. If you ever come by again and have an emergency, please don't hesitate to ring the doorbell. It's programmed to send an alert to my phone." Technically, it was programmed to Chieka's phone since I had a prehistoric brick for a phone, but, details.

"I don't think I should have to ring a bell to get service."

Oh boy. It was going to be like this. I smiled brighter and nodded. "I don't want to waste any more of your time. Where's your car? I'll get that bay door open right away."

She laughed once, without humor. "I would no sooner trust my car to a woman mechanic than I would trust a straight man with my hair." Her fingers brushed over her perfectly styled hair.

I counted to ten in my head, reminding myself not to ball my hands into fists. "Then please, enlighten me as to the honor of your visit."

"I have left you four messages and emailed you as many times about your mother's bridal shower. I knew I simply must have the wrong contact information for you, so I wanted to come by in person so I could update that and we can start planning!"

"Excuse me?" I whispered. I couldn't raise my voice any louder because surely she wasn't asking what I thought she was asking.

She reached out and touched my upper arm. "Us girls are so excited that she's finally found Mr. Right and—"

"No." Was there a more beautiful word in the English language? I didn't think so. "No." I said it again and thrilled at the steel that reinforced my spine. "I can't even believe you would have the audacity to walk into my shop and ask me to throw a bridal shower for my mother, who is marrying my ex."

Amy gasped. "Edith Becker, what has gotten into you? Who cares if you dated him first? That's over and she is your mother!"

"No. She is the woman who gave birth to me. She hasn't been my mother for a long time. Now if you'll excuse me, I have work to do." I went to walk past Amy, but she grabbed my wrist. I twisted out of her grip and held both hands up. "Touch me again and I will call Sheriff Jasmine and file assault charges. Now please leave. You're not welcome in my shop ever again."

Amy's face was so red, it looked like she had a sunburn. "I told Cynthia to keep you out of this shop. It was unnatural and was going to rot your brain. I see it has!"

All of a sudden, Sergeant Cornflakes made a terrifying noise and flew between us like a wrecking ball. I jumped back and snapped my head to the side to find Rosa holding up her phone to record everything. I narrowed my eyes, putting the pieces together. She probably threw the rooster at Amy...not that I was going to be mad, as long as he was okay.

My guard bird was clucking and pecking at Amy's feet while she screamed like a bad horror movie actress. It took everything I had not to burst out laughing. Instead, I stepped forward and picked up my pet before she tried to kick him. She rattled off threats about calling animal control and suing me on her way out of the shop. My bird let out one last crow before struggling out of my hands and waddling over to his tire.

Rosa bent over, laughing so hard she was silent. She lifted her phone and shook it in the air, then pointed at the spot Amy had evacuated. Then she laughed harder.

"I think we broke her!" Tamicka called from the office. I walked over and leaned against the doorframe. She was sitting there with Chieka, eating popcorn. "Is the show over?" Tamicka asked. "It was just getting good."

I studied her. "Do you literally just keep popcorn around, waiting for showdowns?"

She nodded. "Abso-fucking-lutely."

I reached over and grabbed a handful. "That's why I keep you." I nodded to the shop phone on the corner of the desk. "If anyone calls and asks to speak with me and it's not Kristy, Jami, Luke, or an employee, I am absolutely unavailable. They must leave you a detailed message."

Chieka threw a piece of popcorn up in the air and caught it in her mouth, like a badass. "What if it's Ray's telling you they made lasagna?"

I pointed at her. "Good point. Add Ray to that list." I ran my hands over my hair and sighed. "I really hate when people don't trust me because I'm female. Especially another female!"

"Girl, preach," Chieka nodded.

Tamicka lifted her eyebrow. "So what are you gonna do about it?"

I stared at her and frowned. She stared right back at me, slowly eating a piece of popcorn, challenging me. Then, as if my brain was afraid of her look—and to be honest, it was—an idea sprang up out of nowhere. "I'm going to record short videos on how to check things on your car and put them on Instagram."

Tamicka nodded, pointing a red fingernail at me. "There it is. Get to work. I have math to do."

Chieka jumped up and ran around the desk. "My phone's better than yours and I'm pretty sure Rosa is going to need some time to get over her prank. Let's go."

We both looked at Rosa, who was trying to dry the tears still streaming down her face.

"Whatever," I said, but laughter cut off the end of the word. Chieka started laughing, too, and we leaned against each other for support.

"Y'all know you shouldn't drink at work, right?" Tamicka called, but she couldn't hide the amusement in her tone.

When my stomach burned, and my sides hurt, I pushed on Chieka's shoulder and pointed to the door. "Come on," I wheezed. "We'll use your car too."

She put her arm around my shoulder and pumped her other fist in the air. "We're going to be famous!"

"Sure we are. With all ten people who've liked our profile."

She shrugged. "Ten more than we had last week!"

I nodded. "Accurate."

We headed out the back door to the employee parking lot. Chieka's Subaru Outback was parked in the back corner, which would be perfect for filming. She unlocked her car and I paused before popping the hood. "Let's start with how to lift the hood. The basics. Let's get every woman—every person—unafraid of their cars."

Chieka pulled out her phone. "Get ready for Hollywood, Edith Becker!"

WE SHOT small clips well into the afternoon, and for the first time in a long time, I was glad we were slow. It took us a few takes to stop laughing at my awkwardness, and a few more of me stumbling over my words. By the time Ray's delivered lunch, we had gone over the basics that every person who drove a vehicle should know.

Chieka sat next to me at the lunch table and we scrolled through the videos, picking the best ones. "I'll put one up a day with a bunch of hashtags," she said. I had given her the login information Luke had given me.

"Awesome. I'm going to pretend I know what hashtags are. Luke said to use Edie's Auto?"

She shook her head and rolled her eyes. "It's like you're an eighty-year-old man in a twenty-five-year-old's body."

I shrugged. "I take after my grandpa."

Tamicka knocked on the doorframe as she came in.

I eyed her for a long moment before asking the question. "How much more do we need?"

"One hundred forty thousand six hundred dollars and eighty cents."

I groaned and leaned my head against my hand. "How are we going to make that in another week?"

She thrust a piece of paper at me. "I took some liberties."

"Shocking," I replied, taking the paper from her and reading it out loud. "Women, stop being afraid of your car! Come by Edie's Auto for a sixty-minute workshop. Fifty dollars per person, children under twelve free." I looked up at her. "This is genius."

She lifted her eyebrows. "I know!"

"This is...soon. And a lot of postage."

She snatched the paper out of my hand. "Hence why I'm going to see my girl Lindee at the library so she can get me the hookup on copies. Then Rosa, Henry, and I are shoving these into every mailbox in the city."

I stared at her. "T-Money, that's a lot—"

She put her hand up and I shut up immediately, because I valued my life. "Don't want to hear about it. We're your squad. This is our job."

I bit my lip to keep the emotions in.

"If you cry," she warned, "I won't make you Christmas cookies."

I immediately plastered on the biggest smile I could make. Tamicka had promised to learn how to make her amazing cookies Edie-safe and I needed them in my mouth.

She nodded and waved her hand above her head. "See you tomorrow!"

My heart was so full it could burst. Sure, at fifty dollars a head, we wouldn't make much. But it was something and it was proof that these ladies had my back through thick and thin. I shook out my hands and took a deep breath, trying to tamp down the hope blooming in my chest.

Hope, however, was a dangerous thing.

CHAPTER TWENTY-THREE

EDIE'S TIP #30: SOMETIMES THE BEST TRIPS ARE
THE ONES YOU TAKE WITHOUT LOOKING AT THE
MAP...OTHER TIMES YOU JUST GET LOST AND HAVE
TO ASK FOR DIRECTIONS AT THE TACO BELL DRIVE-
THRU AT 2:00 A.M.

BEFORE WE CLOSED ON SATURDAY, Tamicka had given me the good news. "The fliers worked. Every workshop is sold out."

I smiled. "Better add more workshops."

Tamicka put her reading glasses back on and started typing. "I'm emailing the new class dates to every local radio and television station and newspaper. Also, you need to call Uncle Morris."

I stared at her for a long moment until she lifted her eyebrow and everything magically clicked. I smacked myself in the forehead. "I should've done that first thing!"

"Mm-hmm," she replied, turning back to her computer. "You should have. Go do it now."

I pointed at her. "I'll do one better. I'm going for a visit."

It was a short motorcycle ride to the fire station—a fact my home-owner's insurance company loved. I pulled in next to the F-150 whose windshield I had replaced in May. I cringed, realizing that was the last time I'd had a conversation with Uncle Morris. I was going to be in trouble.

I swear, time was running faster and faster every day. Especially for two stubborn people married to their jobs. As I walked toward the open garage door that housed the town's fire engine, a tall and very attractive man stepped out and smiled. He took three giant steps forward and wrapped me in his arms, lifting me off the ground.

"Jack," I wheezed. "Can't breathe, dude."

He laughed and set me down. "Where've they been hiding you, kid?"

"Under a hood, as always."

His huge grin lit up his face. He was white, tall, broad-shouldered, and handsome. The brown freckles that cascaded along his nose and cheeks had darkened with his tan. His reddish-brown hair curled behind his ears, and even I had to admit, it was all *really* working for him.

I sighed, wishing I felt *anything* more than platonic feelings when he smiled. A stomach flip, some butterflies, that damn bat in my chest. Anything.

But alas. "Yo, is your dad around?"

He laughed. "I'm assuming that's a rhetorical question. Yeah, he's in his office. Come on." Jack put his giant arm around my shoulders and led me into the garage. I waved at the chorus of hellos from the other firefighters. We had gotten our first female firefighter this year, which was pretty damn cool.

Jack knocked on Uncle Morris's doorframe before ushering me in. "Look who I found," he said to the older man behind the desk, ignoring the fact that he was on the phone.

White eyebrows shot up to a salt and pepper hairline and Uncle Morris smiled his big, toothy grin. "Ray, gotta call you back. My niece just walked in! Yeah, she is. Bye." He stood and walked around his desk, arms open.

I dashed over and hugged him, a sense of peace washing over me. His hug was a lot like his son's—they were a similar build and probably could bench press about the same. Even though Uncle Morris's hair had turned white, he still looked like he could scare a fire out of a house.

I blinked away the tears that stung the back of my eyes as I realized how starved I had been for a family-like connection. Uncle Morris wasn't really my uncle, but my dad's high school best friend. He'd stepped in and assumed the role as uncle when we were born. It was probably why, much to his dismay, I could never date Jack.

"Jacky, get us some coffees, eh?" Uncle Morris said and then motioned for us to sit in the two chairs in front of his desk. "Tell me what's going on with you, kiddo. You haven't come to visit."

I sat down and rolled my eyes. "You haven't come to visit either. How's the windshield?"

"Good as new as long as I don't put another ladder through her. She's probably got another hundred thousand miles left in her."

Laughing, I said, "If you replace every single part in the car."

He shrugged. "Eh, I like that car. And then you get business."

Jack brought our coffees and set them down. I smiled as he tossed one sugar packet and a stir stick next to my cup. "Thanks, Jack," I said.

Uncle Morris sighed, grabbing his cup and drinking his black coffee like it wouldn't dare burn him. He swallowed and motioned between us. "You sure there's nothing there? I'm getting old. I need grandbabies."

Jack and I exchanged a look and cringed. We had gone out on one date a few months ago after Will and I split. We had a great time, but there was nothing between us but platonic feelings. The kiss was...let's just say, awkward.

"Pa..." Jack warned.

I reached out and grabbed Uncle Morris's arm. "You raised us as family, Uncle Morris. It's a little bit like kissing my cousin."

He shrugged. "Cousins got married all the time in the old days."

Jack shoved his hands in his pockets and shook his head, looking down at me. Faint pink tinted his cheeks. "He's worse than Ma. She at least tries to set me up with the 'nice girls' from church instead of my cousin."

I shoved at Jack's arm. "Go, get out of here before he gets any worse."

Jack laughed, then leaned down and kissed my cheek. "Awesome to see you, Edie." He closed the door on the way out.

I pointed at Uncle Morris. "Don't. Not going to happen in this lifetime."

He looked defeated for a moment and then shrugged. "Hey, a man can try. So, tell me what brings my long-lost niece to visit."

"I need to pull together a very successful fundraiser."

He nodded, reaching for a pad of paper and pen. "Okay, done. When do you want to do this fundraiser? And for whom?"

"Is the end of this week, beginning of next week too early?"

He raised his eyebrows and searched my face. "That's very soon. What's it for?"

I took a big, fortifying gulp of coffee and winced, pretty sure smoke was coming out my nose. "Do you make this with lava?" I choked.

He thumped me once on the back. "Of course. I keep a stash of lava behind the firehouse. Stop trying to sidetrack me."

His tone was playful, but I heard the undercurrent of power in his voice. It was that power that had kept every single firefighter alive over the last ten years. It was that power that raised the funds to keep four full-time firefighters on staff in a town of only fifteen thousand. Most of the small towns surrounding us were volunteer-only.

"The fundraiser is for me."

He stood. "What?! What's wrong? I'll kill that—"

I gripped his arm. "I'm okay! It's for the shop." I briefly wondered whom he would kill, but decided not to ask. Plausible deniability and all that.

Settling back in his chair with his coffee, he motioned for me to continue. So I told him everything—well, almost everything. Nothing about my sex life or Jami's new boyfriend. That was for Jami to share when he was ready.

Uncle Morris was silent for a long moment, taking everything in. "I never liked that boy William. Could never figure out why Cynthia wanted that match so bad. Guess I'm not surprised." He put his mug down on his desk. "I'd always thought there might be something there between you and Luke." He shot me a sideways glance and my cheeks heated.

He pushed himself up from his chair. "Yeah, that's what I thought. He's not my boy, but he's a good one."

I waved my hand in the air, dismissing the notion. "Uncle Morris, he's leaving and—"

He waved his own hand to stop me. "Guys say they're leaving all the time for silly, messed-up reasons. Mark my words, that boy's had it bad for you since you were kids. He'll be back."

I swallowed hard, not daring to hope. "Maybe."

He sat down in his desk chair and picked up the phone. "And if not, my Jacky is still available." I threw my head back and laughed as he dialed a number. "Martha, it's Morris. I need a permit for a fundraiser." He paused. "Saturday?" he asked me. I nodded. There was a loud, shrill response. "Yes, this Saturday." He looked up and winked at me.

My answering grin was so big, it nearly hurt my face. Maybe, just maybe we could do it. Maybe we could save the shop. Maybe Luke would—no. I couldn't even think the words. But my heart beat out a staccato beat to let me know she was thinking the words anyway.

CHAPTER TWENTY-FOUR

EDIE'S TIP #44: AT SOME POINT, YOU'RE GOING TO LOSE YOUR CELL PHONE BETWEEN THE SEATS. WE PROMISE NOT TO LAUGH AT YOU WHEN YOU BRING YOUR CAR IN, PANICKING...BECAUSE WE'VE BEEN THERE TOO.

AFTER SETTLING on a plan with Uncle Morris, I headed back to work to lock up and then walked back home. I stumbled and nearly fell flat on my face when I saw Luke standing in my driveway...in front of my Camaro.

The smile on his face made him look years younger. "Guess what?"

My mouth fell open the moment I connected the dots. Somehow my heap of a car was now sitting in my driveway. Which meant he got the piece to make it run. "How?" I breathed. The part I'd needed was more than I could afford.

He walked up to me and wrapped his arms around me, then gave me a kiss. "I know a guy who owns a couple of junkyards back in North Carolina. Hit him up last week and he came through for me. Got the part today. Chieka helped me sneak in while you were gone."

Tears filled my eyes. "You fixed my car."

He laughed, tightening his hold. "That I did, Reeses. Wanna go for a ride?"

"Do I want to—are you crazy?! OF COURSE I DO!" I ran to the car and caressed her body before opening the door. "Hello, Ella-Jean, my beautiful woman. The love of my life. How are you?"

Luke was smirking as he climbed into the passenger side. He dangled the keys in front of me and I almost ripped off his fingers grabbing at them. "Careful, I need those for later." He winked.

I ignored him and fit the key into the ignition. *Deep breath in, deep breath out.* Then I turned the key.

After a few seconds of tense clicking, the engine caught, and I cheered. It was like she was hugging me with excitement. We buckled up and I backed out of the driveway, turning us toward town. She shook, she rattled, she needed new seats, but she was a dream.

We drove through downtown and looped around, the purr of the engine making me forget about everything except the man next to me. I was sitting next to Luke, holding his hand, while driving Grandpa's car, and everything was *right*.

Then Luke's phone rang.

He pulled it out of his pocket and answered immediately. "Alice May, what's up?"

The carefree, proud man who had been sitting next to me disappeared. In his place was the man whose soul was cut to shreds. "But the baby's okay? That's good, that's good." He pinched the bridge of his nose. "Yeah, bed rest sounds awful. I'm glad your sister is there too." He ran a hand down his face. "Listen, I'm finishing up something. Can I call you later?"

My hands tightened on the steering wheel and I directed the beautiful car back home. Luke hung up and tucked his phone away. "Sorry about that."

I waited a beat, making sure my voice would be steady. "She okay?"

He looked out the window, his hand tapping on the door. "Her doctor put her on bed rest today. Had a bit of a scare. But she's okay. And the baby."

I nodded. "I'm so glad."

As we pulled into the drive, my gut had already told me what I didn't want to admit. With the car running, I could probably get thirty thousand for it. Luke's gift would double what we had saved. I cleared my throat, unable to think about it until he was sound asleep and I was left alone with my thoughts. "Come on. I make a mean scrambled egg for dinner."

CHAPTER TWENTY-FIVE

EDIE'S TIP #22: A ROAD TRIP WITHOUT TUNES IS
LIKE WINE WITHOUT ALCOHOL – POINTLESS AND
UNSATISFYING.

HOW UNCLE MORRIS put this whole thing together in only a few days was mind-boggling. The fundraiser, held in the field between my house and the shop, was almost as fun as the Halloween carnival the town hosted every year. Sure, we didn't have the scary carnival rides that looked like they would topple over in a strong wind, but Ray was there cooking burgers, Celine was slinging coffee, the pie-eating contest had sold out, the Date-A-Firefighter auction was set to start at sunset—I had told Jack to wear his tightest white shirt—and now the oil change competition was about to begin.

Rosa ran up to me, cheeks flushed. "Got the vehicles all lined up for you. Similar makes and models. We've got fifteen entrants."

I motioned for her to lead the way, reaching out to fist-bump Tamicka, who was in charge of the silent auction. Most items were going for under one hundred dollars, but a few, like the weekend trip to a Mackinac Island cabin, were raking in some serious dough. Hell, if I had any money, I'd bid on that too. I couldn't remember the last time I took two days off in a row.

We were charging fifty bucks to enter the oil change contest, winner taking half the pot. Surprisingly, people actually signed up.

Not surprisingly, none of them had ever been to my shop before. This is why they thought they could beat me. Amateurs.

Thanks to volunteers who wanted a free oil change—we would make sure it was done right before they pulled away—we had fifteen sedans parked in a row with the supplies next to them. The contestants mingled, talking trash and bragging about what they would do with the money.

They were all men, except for a fair-skinned, fiery redhead standing off to the side in killer rhinestone sunglasses. Her bright red lipstick matched her fire-engine red capris, which matched her curly hair piled high on her head. I immediately wanted to be her friend.

She leaned on one of the cars, wearing a bored expression, but I could see she was also sizing up her opponents. When one of the guys looked over and asked her what she'd do with the money, she stared at him like he was an idiot. "Give it back to the fundraiser." A silent *duh* rang through the air.

Her answer was met with silence. I liked her. "Who is she? She live here?"

"I think she's just visiting. Name's Vera."

I pursed my lips. "Watch her. I want her." The unspoken words *if we save the shop, if I can hire new people* hung between us.

Rosa gave me a salute. I put my fingers in my mouth and whistled, effectively silencing everyone in a twenty-foot radius. "Hey everyone!" I shouted. "We're going to get under these cars and get dirty! Rosa will have you draw a number and that's your corresponding car. When she blows the whistle"—I pointed to Rosa who held up a little plastic whistle—"we begin."

Everyone drew numbers and found their corresponding car. I got a Honda Civic, a car I could change the oil on with my eyes closed. Luke and Rosa stood together like lifeguards assigned to a toddler swimming class. With her eyes narrowed, Rosa watched us while going over the rules.

"If you take off your safety gear, you're disqualified," she shouted. "If you ask for help from a friend, you're disqualified. If you sabotage another contestant, you're disqualified. When you finish, stand up and raise both hands in the air. We will mark the time and keep the clock going until everyone finishes. Your car will be inspected before a winner is declared!"

She raised the whistle and we all braced ourselves. "On your mark! Get set!" She blew the whistle and I dove in.

A crowd had gathered and started cheering. Cameras were flashing, and fan favorites were getting shout-outs. But I was good at tuning out noise. I had been doing oil changes since I was ten. It was my meditation.

Usually they took me under ten minutes. Today, I was on fire. As the shouting grew louder and louder, I turned my head to the side to catch the words. *Is she going to beat Edie?* I didn't know who'd said it, but I knew I had to burn rubber.

Desperation and determination took over, and I swear I changed that oil faster than any other time in my life. As soon as I finished, I threw both hands in the air only a few seconds before Vera. I bent, doubled over at my waist, and put my hands on my knees, trying to catch my breath. *Holy shit that was close.*

Chieka approached to check out Vera's car. She gave me a thumbs-up while looking suitably impressed.

With a smile, I walked over and extended my hand. "Vera? I'm Edie."

She nodded and took my hand, shaking with a firm grip. "Vera Eastman. It's a pleasure, truly."

"Tell me you live in town and need a job," I begged.

She smirked. "I'm just visiting. I kind of have a gig going right now, but maybe I'll come by the shop soon."

"You do an oil change almost as fast as me. What else can you do?"

She winked at me. "Everything."

Whoa. That wink. Not gonna lie, I had a stomach flutter at that. I definitely was developing a bit of a girl crush. Rosa blew the whistle calling time and I blinked, shaking my head. I walked over to Rosa, Chieka following behind.

Chieka pinched my upper arm. "Is it possible to be straight and be in love with a woman?"

"Girl, I think that I'm a little in love with her too," I muttered.

Rosa glanced up. "With Vera? I already checked. Not single." The three of us all exchanged sad looks. "Anyway, she's probably straight. They always are."

I squeezed her shoulder. "Your woman is out there, *chica*. Be patient."

Luke cleared his throat. "Is this what you women talk about in the shop?"

Rosa shrugged. "Sometimes it's about a car. Or a puppy."

"Or that lemon pie from the bakery," Chieka added.

"We're equal opportunity gushers," I finished.

He just shook his head and wrapped his arms around my shoulders, kissing my cheek. "Proud of you."

I leaned back into him. "Thanks!"

The clearing of a throat had us both turning to see Will standing there, hands on his hips. He was in black dress pants and a white button-down shirt, his "war" uniform. My stomach rolled, and anger filled me.

His eyes were glued to Luke's arms. "From one brother to another?" he sneered. If it had been anyone else saying it, I would have thought it was jealousy.

"From daughter to mother?" I countered.

He shook his head. "Can I talk to you?"

"Isn't that what you're doing?"

"Privately, Edith."

"I'm busy right now." I gestured around the fundraiser. "And I don't want to see you."

"Talk to me and I'll bid on a silent auction item."

I stared at him for a long moment. "You'll bid fifty dollars over the highest bid."

He rolled his yes. "Fine."

I pulled away from Luke, giving him a soft kiss before gesturing to Will. "Two minutes. Talk fast."

Luke held my hand as I walked away, breaking away only when he was forced to let go. I followed Will around to the front of the shop where there were more parked cars than people. I saw my rooster pecking at the corner of one of the bay doors, glad he was staying out of the way. "What do you want?" I asked, stopping by the shop's front door.

He ran his hands through his hair and paced a tight circle. It was his patented uncomfortable pose, the one he did when he didn't want to deal with something. "Cynthia wants you at our wedding," he blurted out.

I stared at him for a long moment. "There is no way in hell I'm going to your wedding." He took a step toward me and I took a step back, both my hands up. "We're done here."

"Please, just listen."

"Why?!"

He threw his hands up in the air and let them fall. "This is why we broke up! You never listened."

"No, we broke up because you started fucking my mother while we were planning our wedding. Or were you just planning hers the whole time?"

He cringed. "I loved you, but she—"

"Don't you dare," I warned.

He ran his hands through his hair again, one of his rolled-up shirt-sleeves starting to droop down his forearm. "I never slept with you after..."

A wave of relief and nausea washed over me. "Thank God," I whispered, hand clutching my stomach. "Now please, get the fuck out of my life."

I turned to walk away. "Just listen to me!" he shouted, grabbing my shoulders from behind. I tensed.

"Let go of me."

He didn't. "You can go back to trying to replace me with my brother in one goddamn minute—"

And I was done. Really done. Years of pent-up anger and resentment collided, and I raised my elbow, then shoved it right into his throat. He let go of me then, gagging, gripping his neck.

I looked up and found Luke running toward me. The moment I was within his reach, he wrapped his arms around me. The safe feeling, the feeling I was *home*, reminded me I wasn't just substituting Luke for Will. Luke was supposed to be my match. I knew it in my bones.

"You okay?" he asked, kissing the top of my head while leading me away.

I nodded, even though I wasn't really. "He said he didn't touch me after sleeping with my mom, so that's a relief."

Luke's jaw clenched, but he forced out a "Small miracles."

He held me tight against him as we walked around the fundraiser, greeting people and directing them toward the area where the auction would begin in fifteen minutes. The noise, the people, the anxiety was almost too much, but Luke's arms were like a blanket on a cold day.

As the crowd swelled, I leaned into him. "Come on, we need to go see if we can oil Jack down to rake in the money."

Luke laughed as we walked toward the makeshift staging area. "I think I might even bid on him." I poked him in the side and he kissed my head, lingering by my ear. "I think you're amazing," he whispered.

A thrill went down my spine. "Yeah?"

He nipped at my ear. "Yeah."

Stay, my brain shouted. *If I'm so amazing, stay!*

I swallowed hard, keeping the words inside as Tamicka picked up the microphone and introduced the firefighters. I didn't shout "stay" while Luke yelled out encouragingly, trying to get people to bid higher. I didn't whisper "stay" in his ear when he picked me up and spun me around when Jack got a three-thousand-dollar bid from Vera, who winked at me as she walked up to pay.

"I think I'm more than a little in love with her," I admitted.

Luke chuckled and kissed me hard.

I didn't get on my knees and beg him to stay, even when he kissed me softly as the crowd dispersed and Tamicka went inside to count the cash. I should have.

CHAPTER TWENTY-SIX

EDIE'S TIP #10: IF YOU SPIN OUT, DON'T FREAK.
STEER INTO THE TURN UNTIL YOU CAN
STRAIGHTEN OUT. THEN PULL TO THE SIDE OF THE
ROAD AND HAVE A GOOD PANIC. WHO DOESN'T
LOVE A GOOD PANIC?

WHILE LUKE, Jack, and Uncle Morris cleaned up, Chieka, Rosa, and I hovered over Tamicka as she finished totaling up the change dropped in the donation cups around the event. She hit a few buttons on the computer, then took off her glasses and rubbed her eyes.

My stomach dropped.

Rosa and Chieka crowded in, each grabbing one of my hands. "T-Money?" My voice cracked, and I cleared my throat. "Tell us."

"We did awesome." The large *but* hovered just over her head. "But we didn't make it."

I was heartbroken. Rosa and Chieka's grips tightened. I swallowed down my dread before I spoke the words that cut like knives. "I'm selling the Camaro for twenty-five thousand." I had no choice but to accept the offer on the Camaro waiting in my email.

Their gasps filled the space between us. Tamicka shook her head. "Girl, Luke fixed that car up for *you*, not for you to sell."

"If I don't save the shop, I have no place to put it anyway. Add that into the total. What do we have?"

She jotted down the numbers and leaned back in her chair. "With the classes, paycheck adjustments, bake sale, car wash, your personal donation, and the Camaro...we still need seventy-five thousand dollars."

White-hot heartbreak spread from the center of my chest to my limbs.

"Ask him if he'll take what we have now. We'll get the rest soon. Somehow."

I shook my head, remembering his story, remembering the pain in his eyes. "I can't ask that of him," I whispered. "If I sell the house, my share of the profit should be enough to save the shop."

Chieka sat on the edge of the desk, hand to heart. "Am I having an out-of-body experience? Are you crazy? You can't sell your house."

I shrugged. "It's just a house." What a load of bullshit that was. I didn't know if I said it for her benefit or my own.

"We still have time," Tamicka stated. "Until his fine ass is in that truck and driving away, we have time. Let's go home and rest tonight. Tomorrow we'll try again. Okay?"

We all nodded.

Rosa sighed. "I'm going to go take videos of Sergeant Cornflakes."

Chieka gave me a quick hug, kissed my cheek, then left without a word.

My phone buzzed, and I cringed when the text popped up.

Luke: Did we do it?!

I closed my eyes. I loved Luke. My beautiful, grieving man who was just trying to do right by his friend's widow. "I'll call the realtor in the morning," I told Tamicka.

Before she could argue with me, I grabbed my small purse from the top desk drawer and walked out of the shop. I texted Luke back.

Me: We are super close!!

It wasn't necessarily a lie. My phone buzzed, and Luke had sent me a dozen exclamation marks. I shoved it back into my pocket and looked up at my home, lit by my porch light. Like my grandparents, I had always assumed I would live in this house until I died.

I tried to memorize the way it looked in twilight, the feeling of peace that settled over me whenever I walked up the path. My Camaro sat in the driveway around the side of the house and I walked over to her to say goodbye.

Tears threatened, but I shoved them down. *It's only stuff. You can't bring Grandpa back with a car. Grandma isn't inside baking your favorite pie.* If only logic worked on emotions. I climbed into the driver's seat and closed the door. My hands ran over the steering wheel. "I'm sorry I can't keep you," I whispered to her.

I startled when the passenger side door opened and Luke slid in. "Why am I not surprised that you're celebrating with your car?"

I forced a smile. "Because you know me too well." I was thankful for the dark because I was a terrible actress. If he had seen me in full light, I wouldn't have been able to pull it off.

"This feels a bit like my first night back in town," he teased. "And I still really want you to lean over and kiss me."

My head snapped to look at him. "You wanted me to kiss you then?"

He reached up and trailed his fingers down my jaw. "Yeah." I swallowed hard and he leaned forward so our lips were only inches apart. "One moment, you were talking about being cake-blocked. Then next thing I knew..." His eyes met mine and held, and he waited for me to take control.

Taking my cue, I leaned in and pressed my lips to his.

This time, he did respond. His hand buried in my hair, holding my mouth against his. He parted his lips, his tongue brushing against my bottom lip before he deepened the kiss. The air was charged around us, my skin burning bright in the dark.

Somehow I got on his side of the car without smashing my head on anything, although if I were an inch taller, I'd hit the roof. My knees barely fit on either side of his hips. But we kissed and kissed and kissed, the drag of his stubble burning the skin around my lips. I didn't care, I needed more of him. *Please never forget this,* I begged my brain.

He wrapped his arms around my waist and pulled me hard against his erection. I groaned, breaking our kiss, my head tipping back. His mouth took over caressing my neck, nibbling across my collarbone, and I slowly melted into him.

He tugged at my shirt and I took it off, tossing it onto the driver's seat. He pulled the cups of my bra to the side and took my pebbled nipple into his mouth, sucking hard. An electrical shock went from my breast to between my legs, and I ground harder against him.

By the time he kissed his way to my other nipple, sweat was misting out of my skin. My feelings were threatening to spell out every time I took a breath. *I love you, stay, I love you, stay, I love you*, my brain wanted to shout. Instead, I ran my fingers all over him.

Everything was supercharged in this small, enclosed space surrounded by darkness. Maybe it was because I knew I was losing him, was losing this car, losing this place. Maybe it was because this was what I'd wanted to happen the first night I kissed him. Maybe it was because I was tired of fighting against my feelings.

I bent my face down to his neck and whispered into his salt-tanged skin, "I need you."

He groaned and reached down to unbutton his jeans, then stopped. "Shit." He dropped his hands and leaned back in the seat. "We used my wallet condom last night and I totally forgot to put a new one in."

I rotated my hips, dragged his length against my center, making us both temporarily forget everything but the places where we touched. Luke groaned my name. "We need to get inside."

I stopped him with a kiss. Reaching my arm out to find my purse, I dumped the entire thing out onto the empty seat and pulled out a condom. "Make love to me in this car."

My heart beat hard against my ribs. This would be a memory between us, one that I would carry with me until I was an old lady. I knew when he left, he was taking my heart with him. I selfishly wanted him to think of this moment for the rest of his life too.

I lifted up and unbuttoned my shorts, pushing them and my

underwear down with some mild contorting. His breath was shaky as he undid his jeans and shoved them and his boxers down to his mid-thighs. Ripping open the foil wrapper with my teeth, I pulled out the latex and pinched the tip before slowly rolling it down his shaft.

By the time I had finished, he looked like he had endured something. "Turn around," he growled, putting his hands on my hips and helping me maneuver in the small space.

Once my back was to him, he pulled me hard against his chest. He kissed the spot where my neck and shoulder met as he gripped his erection and slid it back and forth against my clit, making sparks of pleasure dance along my skin. The anticipation of having him, of feeling him inside of me, was making an invisible band of need tighten around my lungs.

"Luke," I whispered, twisting my head back so I could kiss his mouth.

"Reeses." He smiled against my lips. Then he shifted our bodies, placed himself at my entrance, and slowly eased in.

The feeling of him in this position, in this car, nearly in public was intoxicating. It was the thrill of driving a motorcycle after a lifetime of walking, times ten. He moved us in a slow and steady rhythm, burying his forehead against me. "Edith," he whispered. "Edith, Edith, Edith."

The way he said my name was reverent as he deepened his strokes. His hands were iron bars wrapped around me, holding me to him. My head was bent backward, resting against his as each movement tightened something inside of me unlike any other time before. This feeling was bigger, more important, more devastating.

Stay, my mind shouted. *Stay, stay, stay.* His hand moved down my body to my clit and he began rubbing as he moved inside of me and I was lost. I would've done anything he asked. Jump, tap dance, fly. Anything.

I opened my mouth, words pushing out without my permission. "Luke, I love you." I tensed as the words registered.

He kissed everywhere he could reach on me. "I love you," he whispered against my skin. "Love you, love you."

It was as if he lit a firework inside of me. I gripped his thighs and ground down, taking him harder. His hand moved faster and with his name on my lips, I broke apart. A silent scream bowed my back and he pulled me hard against him as he groaned into the back of my neck before pumping hard and throbbing his release inside of me.

My orgasm kept going, my limbs vibrating with leftover pleasure. His fingers stroked up and down my arms. As our panting turned to regular breathing, and our sweat-misted skin dried, we reluctantly separated.

I pulled on my underwear and his T-shirt before getting out of the car. He pulled up his pants and followed me into the house where we both stripped down again and got in the shower, making love again. I didn't worry about tomorrow, about the heartbreak that was just around the corner.

I just made sure to keep telling him how I felt over and over again with my lips, hands, and body. As we faced each other, drowsy, and kissing softly, I wished I had the guts to say that one extra word.

Stay.

CHAPTER TWENTY-SEVEN

WHEN MY EYES finally forced themselves open, I stretched, my arm going to Luke's side of the bed and finding it empty. His pillow was cool to the touch. Sitting up, I looked around, unable to explain the twisting in my stomach. He wasn't in the bedroom or bathroom.

Tugging on his T-shirt and a pair of sleep shorts, I went downstairs and found him searching for something. "Morning," I said cautiously.

"Have you seen my phone?" he asked, a little panicked.

I frowned and shook my head. "Maybe it fell out of your pocket in the Camaro?" For some reason, the memory of the car made my face heat. It was probably how detached he seemed right now. I knew he kept his phone on him in case Alice May needed anything, and I respected his concern. They had both just lost someone they cared about very much.

But this was different. I grabbed my keys out of the bowl by the door and tossed them to him. "What's wrong?"

He shoved a hand through his hair. So much like Will, yet so different. "I just...I don't know. My gut says something is wrong."

After his time in the service, I knew that gut feeling was what kept him alive this long.

My stomach tightened as I watched him jog to the car, open the door and run his hand along the seats. He pulled the phone out from underneath the seat and jolted when he saw the screen, dropping the keys. Not bothering with shoes, I ran out after him as he lifted the phone to his ear.

His face was contorted with guilt and anguish. "I'll be there as soon as I can." He hung up and pressed his palms to his forehead, breathing heavy.

I approached him like a wild animal, with my hands in the air. "Luke, come on. I'll help you pack."

He shook his head, angry tears making his eyes shine. "She went into labor last night. It's too early. Her sister's been calling me all night. They're afraid—"

I wrapped myself around him as he fell apart, burying his face in my neck. "Shhh, shhh," I soothed, rubbing his back.

"How am I supposed to do this? How can I walk away from us? How can I leave her alone?"

I pulled back and looked up at him. My heart tried to crawl out of my throat, wanting to escape the damaging blow I was about to give it. "You can't stay, Luke. You made a promise."

"But what about us?" he whispered.

"We were never supposed to be an 'us.' We both knew this was temporary." I shrugged with apparent nonchalance. "It was fun though, while it lasted."

The words cut him exactly how they needed to. He took a step back, anger replacing the heartache of leaving. I pointed to the front door. "I'm going to go cut your check, and I'll start some coffee while you pack." Without a word, I ran back into the house, gripping my chest, trying to keep it from collapsing in on my lungs.

I ran the tasks through my head over and over again, trying to focus on them. I found my company checkbook and wrote a check for every last cent I could give him. I was still short, but with the way the housing market was, I had no doubt I could wire the rest of the money soon.

I started the coffee and pulled down my best travel mug. I filled a cooler with some ice packs, bottles of water, and leftovers. I threw in a few bananas and granola bars for good measure. It was all just a few less things I'd have to eventually pack.

Luke burst through the door, slamming it and stomping up the stairs. I heard my furniture moan in protest as he manhandled the drawers to pull his clothes out. I gripped the edge of the counter, reminding myself to breathe. It was better this way.

The coffee machine beeped and I filled the travel mug, carrying it and the cooler to the door. Luke careened down the stairs with a duffle bag slung over his shoulder. He stopped right in front of me and I swallowed hard, unable to look into his eyes. I took a deep breath, trying to memorize the way he smelled one last time.

I gave him the check. "When the pledges come in, I'll send you the rest." I didn't want him to know about the house yet. Not when he could see the pain in my eyes. Not when I could still see the guilt in his.

"So those words you whispered to me last night?" he asked, desperate. "Edith, what if—"

"Heat of the moment, you know," I interrupted before he changed everything. I knew if he stayed, he'd resent me. The guilt would eat us alive and it would be my relationship with my mother all over again. She'd resented me my entire life. I couldn't take it if Luke ever looked at me the way she did.

"You can't tell me we don't have something amazing," he said.

I shrugged. "Maybe it was because we both knew it wasn't going to last." I was going to throw up everything I had ever eaten. I wanted to fall to my knees and beg him to stay forever. Tell him I would love him until the end of time. *Stay, stay, stay.*

His jaw tightened, and he nodded once. "I see. Well. Fooled me." He adjusted his bag on his shoulder and took the check from my hand. "Take care of yourself, Edie."

He moved to push past me out onto the front step and I shoved the cooler and travel mug into his hand. "Here, take these. It's a long trip." I made the mistake of looking in his eyes and I knew if I didn't run back inside that very moment, my façade would fail me. It was only working because he was so distressed.

"Have a good trip!" I said too cheerfully, then ran back into the house and locked the door. I listened for his truck to start and then strained to hear the sound as it pulled out of the driveway, taking my heart with it.

CHAPTER TWENTY-EIGHT

WHEN JAMI BARGED in a week later, I was on my fifth viewing of *Dirty Dancing* while wearing a shirt Luke had left behind. I was also eating ice cream out of the container because all of my bowls were dirty. Quite frankly, I wasn't even sure how clean the spoon was, but who cares?

Jami looked around the living room, inhaled, cringed, then stomped over and ripped the ice cream out of my hand.

"Hey!" I shouted, hitting him with a throw pillow.

He grabbed it and hit me right back. "How long has it been since you showered?"

I ripped the pillow out of his hand and threw it behind the couch. "GO AWAY. No one wants you here."

He eyed me carefully before he dumped the container on the coffee table, then stomped upstairs. I heard the shower turn on and I wiggled my butt into the couch, trying to sink deeper. Crossing my arms, I shot fire from my glare as he reappeared. He didn't seem to give a damn as he bent down and picked me up in a firefighter's hold.

"What are you doing, you crazy person?!" I yelled, banging on his back.

He smacked my ass. "Calm down, psycho. You've got a dozen women in your shop right now waiting for your class and you're not there. Chieka started with the basics, but they came to see you."

He walked me straight into the bathroom, pulled off my slippers, and dumped me, clothes and all, into the shower. I screamed bloody murder, but he slammed the door. "If you come down unshowered, I will pour all your wine down the sink!" he yelled.

"Fuck you!" I retorted.

"That's Caden's job!"

I had never showered with such anger. I scrubbed my scalp until it tingled and shaved twice because I missed two hairs. But the hot water was magic and suddenly, I started feeling like a human again. Well, three-quarters of a human.

Remembering there were people waiting for me at the shop, I sped through the end of my shower and braided my wet hair. I still looked like I'd been hit by a truck, but at least flies weren't buzzing around me anymore.

When I finally came downstairs, I smelled coffee and toast. I was shocked to see that Jami had cleaned my kitchen. He turned around when I entered and pointed to the bar where a plate of peanut butter toast and a cup of coffee waited. "Eat. Drink."

I nodded and slid across the floor, staring at the toast. I picked it up and inspected it as though I had never seen toast before. For the first time in days, my stomach growled, announcing it was finally ready for solid food. I inhaled the toast and coffee, and Jami immediately washed the dirty dishes.

"I swear you've used every dish in this house." He cringed. "At least go paper if you aren't going to clean. You'll get flies."

I rolled my eyes. "Okay, Grandma."

He pointed his sponge wand at me. "Damn straight. Now go away. I'm going to start laundry, because if you were eating cereal out of coffee mugs, I don't even want to think about your underwear situation."

I ran to him and gave him a kiss on his cheek. He pushed back and gave me a shove toward the door. "When you're done, we'll take another load of stuff over to my place, okay?" he called.

I gave him a thumbs-up and ran out the door, trying to ignore the For Sale sign in my front yard. Thankfully, the two viewings we'd had were the day after Luke had left, before it looked like a natural disaster had rolled in. Heartbreak does that to a person.

When I entered the shop, everyone turned to stare at me. Chieka recovered first and motioned her hand toward me. "And now that we've learned how to change our headlights, Edie is going to take over."

She walked over to me and gave me a quick hug. "We changed a tire, headlight lamp, and windshield wipers."

I clapped my hands and pointed to the truck with the open hood. "Up next, let's talk about windshield washer fluid and checking your oil!"

As the women gathered around, I fell back into my groove, my heartache taking a back seat to my love of teaching others about their cars. For forty minutes, we went over the car from headlights to taillights and the students all posed for a picture around me at the end, holding up the course completion certificates Tamicka had printed.

"That's going on Instagram," Chieka said, quickly tapping buttons on her phone. "And let's add a filter because, girl, you look like a ghost."

Tamicka leaned out of her office after the shop emptied, gave me a once-over, and shook her head. "You're a damned fool," she said, crossing her arms.

I sighed and took a step forward. "T-Money—"

She held up her hand. "You finally find a man you love more than *stuff* with memories, you hang onto that man, come hell or high water. You go with him if you need to. You beg him to stay."

I put my hands on my hips. "How do you know I didn't beg him to stay?" I shouted, defiantly. I hadn't asked him, but that wasn't the point right now.

She turned around, attitude in every sharp movement she made. "Because he would still be here. And you wouldn't look like you just made the worst mistake of your life." With that, she slammed the office door and went back to her computer.

Chieka sucked in a breath through her teeth. "Yowza."

"Am I good to go home?" I asked.

She pointed toward the door. "Get outta here, you look like shit. Get some sleep. See you tomorrow." She kissed my cheek and then smacked my butt as I walked away.

CHAPTER TWENTY-NINE

EDIE'S TIP #8: MAKE SURE TO GET YOUR BRAKES
CHECKED. NOTHING IS MORE EMBARRASSING THAN
TRYING TO CHECK OUT A HOT GUY AND THEN
HEARING A SCREEEEEEECH. OR, YOU KNOW,
HITTING THE CAR IN FRONT OF YOU. NOT THAT I
KNOW FROM PERSONAL EXPERIENCE...NOPE...

MOVING SUCKED. A week after my sold-out workshop, I was struggling to carry two overfull boxes out when someone grabbed the screen door for me. I stopped dead when I saw Will holding it open, two to-go cups of coffee in his other hand. He looked up at me, his aviators reflecting my hesitation.

I set the boxes down on the porch and stepped away from the door. He let it swing closed, then cautiously extended a coffee to me. "Celine said you take one sugar." When I didn't move to take the cup, he rolled his eyes. "It's not poisoned, I promise."

I paused for a few beats before accepting the cup. "Are you sure?"

He shrugged one shoulder, a gesture so like Luke my stomach twisted. "I deserved the throat punch."

I nodded, then motioned to the front door. "Wanna come in?"

He motioned to the step. "Why don't we sit out here. Just give me one moment." I sat down, and he set his coffee next to me, then walked over to the For Sale sign. With one yank, he pulled it out of the ground and laid it down on the grass. Tears stung my eyes as I struggled to take a deep breath.

Someone had offered.

I needed to go to the hardware store to get more boxes. Then I had to forward my mail and double-check where the property line ended. I would have to build a fence around the shop, assuming the bid was high enough for me to buy out Luke and Will.

Anxiety clawed the inside of my stomach. I glared at the offensive sign on my lawn for a few long moments, then took a long sip of coffee, swallowing hard. I didn't really care if it was poisoned anymore.

Will walked back to the stoop and sat down. "You should consider remodeling the shop. Maybe expanding to add a coffee bar." He took off his sunglasses and tucked them into the front of his shirt, then stared at me.

I opened my mouth, but no words came out. My gaze went from my coffee cup to him a few times before I managed, "I'm so confused right now. Are you sure this isn't poisoned? Laced with hallucinogens?"

His gaze held mine for a long moment. "I know that we turned to shit. Doesn't mean I don't care. But sometimes, I'm a jackass."

"Sometimes?" I muttered.

He just glared at me. "Don't. You were right; we didn't work. And I should've talked to you, ended it earlier. But you aren't blame-free here."

Shame, anger, and exhaustion all warred in my chest, making my neck hot. "Why are you here, Will?" I sighed. "This day is hard enough." *Now that Luke is gone. Now that my home is gone.*

"I'm here to let you know that Sara pulled the house off the market."

There was only one residential real estate office in town, and it was Will's company. While I'd used his associate, I wasn't surprised he knew about it. He and Cynthia were really made for each other with their love of real estate and their obsession with sticking their noses in everyone's business.

Don't cry. Don't cry. "When do I need to be out?"

He took a deep breath. "You don't."

I stared at him, blinking rapidly. "Um...what?"

"The morning Luke left, Jami showed up at my door and..." He rubbed his jaw. "Let's just say we had a heart-to-heart. I didn't know the whole story about what happened with Luke."

He looked down at his shoes for a moment, like he did when he was embarrassed. "So." He ran a hand through his hair. "I started a FundMePlease campaign to raise money for his buddy's family. You and I both know Luke is too proud to do it himself. A few online papers reposted it and the campaign made fifteen thousand."

He closed the distance between us and grabbed the coffee cup out of my hand, setting both of ours down. "It also got a huge, anonymous thirty-five thousand dollar donation yesterday. From someone in Grenadine."

I gasped.

He put his hands on my shoulders and turned me toward him. "I'm paying you back all the deposits for the wedding and for your dress. That's another ten thousand. That brings you to sixty thousand."

"I'm still fifteen thousand short," I choked out. I was nauseated. Would I ever wake up from this nightmare? I just wanted it to be done.

He squeezed my shoulders, which was such a Luke thing to do. "Luke said he'd take it and call it even. I wired the money this morning. Call Jami and he'll tell you that Luke and I electronically signed the entire parcel over to you an hour ago. Which means...you don't need to sell. It's all yours—the shop, the house, and the land, one hundred percent."

I covered my face with my hands and lowered my head to my knees, sobbing. "W-Will..." I couldn't finish the sentence.

He crouched down in front of me. "This is the way it always should've been. This was your dream, Edith."

My hands dropped. I looked up into the familiar brown eyes, and for the first time in nearly a year, I felt something other than disgust. Maybe grudging respect? "Why did you do this?" I whispered. "I'm your ex."

"Edith, he's my big brother. I love him. I'd do almost anything for him."

I took a shuddering breath, blinking rapidly. "This is totally out of left field." I narrowed my eyes. "Are you high?"

"No." His jaw clenched.

"What about Cynthia? Does she know?" I ran a hand through my hair to hide its shaking. "Giving me my dreams means she doesn't get hers."

He nodded. "She'll be okay. We'll be okay." He rubbed his hands over his face. "You two are so much alike, but there's just so much baggage between you, you don't see it."

"I don't know about that." I laughed without humor.

"You're both strong, determined women who know what they want and do what they need to get it." He finally met my gaze. "She's you in eighteen years, Edith. And as someone who lost his mother way too young, I hope you two figure out how to get along."

"Will—"

He held up his hand. "I know I played a role in this discord, and I am truly sorry. We would love to have you at our wedding, but if you don't want to come, I completely understand. I just hope we can figure out how to all be in the same room someday." He brushed nonexistent lint off his pants. "I really miss big family holidays."

"Me too," I admitted.

He sighed and sat back down next to me. "Luke stopped by Dad's on the way out of town. I was there." He shoved his hands into his hair. "You know I get so fixated on things, like this wedding and Cynthia and just, trying to make everything work—" He blew out a hard breath. "While Luke's gone, it's easy to forget how much I miss him. How I don't even know him anymore. He's the only family I've got left."

I reached over and gripped his forearm. "Will..."

"No one else remembers what Christmas morning was like when both our parents were healthy. No one else knows how he held my hand when he walked me to school in first grade or beat up the older kids who tried to take my lunch. No one else remembers what it was like to go with Dad to the Lions game every Thanksgiving. No one else knows how hard it is to miss Mom in the quiet moments."

His chin rested in his hand and he turned to face me, although his eyes didn't meet mine. "Luke looked so tired, so damn exhausted and homesick. I am too. Mom's gone; Dad's basically gone. I can't lose my brother again too. Cynthia gets why I have to do this."

Realization was like a punch to the gut. "She lost both of her parents, too," I whispered. We were both silent for a long moment, wrapped up in our own thoughts.

He cleared his throat. "Maybe now that Alice May has had her baby, things will settle down. Her bills are taken care of...I don't know. Maybe Luke will come back. Especially if the woman he loves is waiting for him." He smiled softly. "And he loves you."

I shook my head. "I fucked it all up."

His eyes found mine. "You love fiercely; it's one of your best qualities. And you love him, more than you ever loved me. There's no way he could stay away, trust me." He helped me stand as I opened my mouth to argue.

He held up his finger. "Don't argue. We imploded because of this house. It was one of the reasons I struggled so hard in our relationship. I always felt like all this"—he gestured around us—"came first and I was a consolation prize."

"Will..." I whispered in apology, shame coloring my cheeks. He was right. I wouldn't have given up the house for him, ever. "We should've talked about it."

"Yeah." He shrugged. "Anyway, I'm sorry about...everything. But you have to know how happy Cynthia makes me. She puts me first."

I tried not to cringe. Or barf in my mouth. "That's...good," I lied. It was still really fucking weird. "I'm never calling you *Dad*."

He groaned. "Please don't. It's weird enough. My ex is going to be my stepdaughter and my sister-in-law."

I shook my head. "Okay, get out of here before I throw up on your shoes."

He laughed and put on his sunglasses. "Yeah, yeah." He reached out his arms out for a hug.

I held up my hand. "We aren't there yet. But...thanks." I held out my hand and he shook it in both of his. When he let go, I raised an eyebrow and cocked my head. "Sister-in-law?"

"He's told me he's been in love with you since we were kids. If he doesn't put a ring on it, *I'll* punch *him* in the throat for you." He took a few steps back. "Seriously, Edie. We'll get him home. Then we both win."

CHAPTER THIRTY

EDIE'S TIP #19: ALWAYS CARRY A SPARE, OR YOU'LL
END UP SEEING ME. WHICH IS ACTUALLY NOT A BAD
THING; I'M A DELIGHT!

I STARED AT MY PHONE. Then I stared at it some more. I restarted it twice. Still nothing. No new calls, texts, or emails.

Luke's phone had gone straight to voicemail the last seven times I tried to call, and I couldn't leave a message because the mailbox was full. Outside of a picture message of his new godson, Alberto Jr., I hadn't heard from him since he'd left almost three weeks ago. Well, twenty days, four hours, sixteen minutes, and seven seconds.

I had to do something, even if it meant losing him forever. So, after a generous helping of tea, I'd spilled my guts to a computer screen. One last email. No alcohol, just truth.

I told him about the house, about what Will had done, about how sorry I was for being too afraid to ask him to stay. I told him about this amazing idea I had to drive around to different universities and teach a weekend seminar on car basics. I told him I loved him.

Then, without even proofreading it, I sent it.

I proceeded to spend the next three days rereading it in a constant state of shock and panic. I didn't know what I was expecting from the email. It wasn't like he'd ever responded to one before.

My phone rang and I dropped it, screaming. I dove for it and answered before it even got to my ear. "Hello! Hello?" I gasped into it, not even bothering to check who was calling.

"Uh," my brother said. "Are you okay, sissy?"

I sank onto my couch. "Yeah, just running up the stairs to finish packing for my trip." Lies. I'd finished packing an hour ago and was now just waiting for my lunch to cook before I took off.

"Liar, I know you finished packing an hour ago. Listen, you sure you won't regret not coming to the wedding?"

I guffawed. "I would rather clean the bathroom with my toothbrush naked while being bitten by fire ants."

There was a long pause. "That's oddly specific. But okay. Have fun and drive safe."

"I can't believe you're actually going. I can't believe you agreed to be *in* the wedding!"

He chuckled. "Yeah, yeah. But I'm bringing a date."

I choked on air, my hand pounding my chest to get my lungs working right. "You're taking Caden?!" I wheezed. "You're coming out to Mom at her wedding?!"

"You wanna come now, don'tcha?" he teased.

"Yes, I want to be a fly on the wall."

He laughed. "I'll have Kristy send you the video. Promise. This is her revenge too."

"You're the best big brother a girl could ask for." The buzzer for my stove went off and I jumped up to grab my gluten-free pizza. "Okay, this girl's gotta eat and hit the road. South Haven won't come to me."

"Text me when you get there, and have a good time, okay? Love you, little sis!"

"Love you, big bro."

MY BAG WAS TIED to the back of my motorcycle and I was decked out in my full-face helmet and thick riding gear when Chieka ran up the path, waving her arms. I pulled my helmet off and sighed. I knew I shouldn't have shut my phone off. "What?"

Chieka shrugged apologetically. "Girl, I'm so sorry, but I can't get ahold of Earl and there's someone down at Freemont and Porter that needs a tow."

I growled. "Seriously?!" It would take me at least forty-five minutes to get out there, hook them up, and bring them back to the shop. I knew I should've left earlier and eaten on the road. So much for beating the traffic.

"I'm sorry."

I pulled off my gear and tossed it on top of my bike, then motioned for her to lead the way. I snatched a clean set of coveralls and put them on over my jeans, tying them around my waist. I'd dressed for comfort and a long bike ride this morning, so my hair was in a messy ponytail and my bra strap kept threatening to fall down my arm. This was definitely not my most professional look, but I wasn't going to take the time to change, and I didn't want to get dirty. Chieka tossed me the keys for the truck and I ran out back, started the beast up, and burned rubber out of the driveway.

Okay, I didn't actually burn rubber, the thing was massive, but I drove with determination. My annoyance filled the silent cab as I made the turn down Freemont. I was hoping it was just a dead battery that I could jump and send them straight to the shop without having to tow. Wishful thinking and all.

My heart leaped into my throat as a black Explorer came into view with its hood up. I shook my head hard. I knew it wasn't Luke. There were hundreds of black Explorers in this town.

A guy in dark jeans and a white T-shirt leaned over the engine. A guy with the exact same silhouette as Luke. I barely managed to get the truck pulled over as I began hyperventilating. It couldn't be him. He was in North Carolina.

It took me three tries to get the door open, my hands were shaking so much. I took a deep breath and steadied myself. I could do this. It was just some man who looked like Luke and had his style truck. It was bound to happen, even in a small town.

But as I approached, the man turned around and I stopped dead in my tracks. Luke stood there, arms crossed, smiling so big I forgot how to breathe. "She just stopped running. Figured I'd better get it towed in."

I stood there, frozen, every word in my email coming back. *I love you. I honestly think it's always been you. I wish I'd begged you to stay.*

"I got your email," he said. "I decided to respond in person."

That damn bat in my chest resuscitated itself and started flapping like crazy. "Wha...how?"

He took a step toward me but stopped as my eyes widened. "Alice May decided to sell her house and move to Florida with her sister. When she learned about you, she promptly chased me around the house with a shoe until I promised I'd go live my own life."

"Your job?"

He shrugged. "My heart hasn't been in it for a long time. I quit. And now I'm jobless. You still hiring? I'm pretty good at car stuff."

I opened and closed my mouth, but nothing came out. I just nodded instead.

"The moving truck was already loaded when you sent that email. I'm back for good. My stuff will be here in a week."

I nodded, still in shock. "So, your truck?" I pointed to the tow truck behind me, ignoring how my voice wavered.

He smiled. "She won't run."

My cheeks were probably scarlet, and I kept my eyes on his truck, too afraid to look at him. A quick glance over the engine made me shake my head. I turned around and leaned back on my elbows against the Explorer. "You know what would make your truck run better? If you reconnected the battery."

He nodded seriously. "Ah, I wondered if that might be important. I appreciate you coming out to check." He took a step forward and put his right arm on the hood, above my head, bringing us close.

My stomach dropped to the center of the earth. "I'm sorry for what I said before you left," I admitted. "I was just saying what I thought you needed to hear."

"Yeah?"

I nodded. "I love you. Please stay." My heartbeat was so loud in my ears, I almost couldn't hear him.

"I see." He took another step forward, his hand going to my chin and keeping our gazes locked. "That's great, because I love you too. And I'm here to stay, if you'll have me."

"Promise?" I whispered.

"Always." He took another step into me. "I think the idea of you traveling around and teaching people about their cars is brilliant. I would love to travel with you."

I bit down hard on my bottom lip so I didn't start crying. My chest was clogged with a hundred bats all fluttering at once. "But you said this place could never be your home."

His hand smoothed around to the back of my neck. "Any place where you're not in my arms isn't home. Because you're my home."

I couldn't stop the two tears that escaped out the sides of my eyes. He leaned in and kissed them away, then his mouth hovered just above my lips. "I love you, Reeses."

"I love you too."

His lips pressed to mine and we wrapped our arms tightly around each other. My knees buckled as he deepened the kiss, and he scooped me up, holding me against him. By the time he pulled away, I was laughing with pure joy.

He placed light kisses all over my face, brushing my hair behind my ears. "I can't believe you were going to sell the house for me."

I shrugged. "I would've done anything for you."

He smirked. "I knew it. I so knew it!"

I poked him. "Come on, I'm going to a bed and breakfast for the weekend. Want to come with?"

He nodded and then pursed his lips. "Yes, conditionally." I raised my eyebrow. He walked over to the truck and opened the door, pulling out a furry, sleeping bundle. "Do they allow pets?"

"What?!" I asked, running over. A sleepy French bulldog puppy with a bandaged paw blinked his big eyes at me. "Who is this?" I asked, my voice going incredibly high.

"This is Dash," he said. "Found him on the side of the road on my way back here. He had no tags and no microchip. Had been on his own for a few weeks, the vet said."

I scooped Dash into my arms and held his warm little body against mine. He was wiggling in excitement and licking my face. "Oh my gosh, he's the cutest!" I smiled up at Luke.

He leaned down and kissed me, slow and deep until Dash gave a small bark. Luke laughed, pulling away. "Oh, you gonna get jealous every time I kiss your mommy, huh?" The puppy barked in answer as if he understood.

I laughed, handing him back Dash. "I'll reconnect the battery and you can follow me home."

He looked back to me, eyebrows raised. "Home?"

I crossed my arms. "If you think you and Dash aren't moving in with me, I will punch you in the throat."

He laughed. "Well, I'd better not argue with you, then."

I narrowed my eyes at him. "The dog was your backup plan, wasn't he? If I was on the fence about it, you were going to have him woo me with his cute old-man face, weren't you?"

He winked, and my heart skipped a beat. "I'll never tell."

With one last kiss, he put Dash back into his truck while I reattached the battery and closed his hood. I was practically bouncing up and down on the seat as we drove back to the shop. Once I had parked and shoved the keys into the shop's mailbox, I ran up the driveway to find Luke pulling Dash out of his truck and setting him down. "Welcome home, buddy!"

He immediately dashed off toward the coop and I put my hand to my mouth. "Oh God, he's not going to eat Sergeant Cornflakes, right?"

At the sound of his name, my rooster came out and crowed loudly, flapping his wings. Dash let out a low whine and took several steps back, and I burst out laughing. Luke walked over and wrapped me in his arms. "I don't think it's going to be a problem."

Dash ran circles around my chicken, trying to get him to play. The puppy was so fast, he was a blur. "I see where he got his name!" I said, laughing.

"He's going to give us a run for our money."

Us. Our. My stomach squeezed at those words. As if sensing what I was feeling, Luke held me tighter as I nuzzled my face into his neck. "Stay," I said simply.

"Always."

EPILOGUE

LUKE and I were snuggled together watching a movie in our hotel room—a hotel where pets were allowed—when my phone started vibrating off the nightstand. I grabbed it and sat up, scrolling through the cascade of messages from Kristy, Sam, and Jami. I laughed and covered my mouth as I tried to catch up with the group text.

Luke sat up, kissing my spine on the way. My stomach flipped even though we had been wrapped in each other the entire evening. "What's going on?" he asked, brushing my hair to the side and kissing my neck.

"Jami just came out at my mother's wedding!"

Luke pulled back and laughed, then put his chin on my shoulder to read the messages along with me.

Kristy: Jami just came out @ wedding!

Sam: Holy shit bro that was beautiful

Kristy: Payback's a bitch

Sam: Hold on I have video...

Jami: Thank you, thank you. I thought it was poetic justice.

Sam: [Video]

I hit play. Jami was giving a speech into the microphone when he lifted his glass. "Now, I know it's my mother and William's day," he said. "But I believe they would be as happy for me as I am for them!"

I covered my face with my hand. "Oh God, he did it. I can't believe he did it!"

"This afternoon, this amazing man, my boyfriend, Caden, told me he loved me, and I said it back! So from one happy couple to another, congratulations, Mom and William!"

Kristy: FIERCE!

Sam: Aunt Cynthia is mortified. It's amazing.

Jami: [Picture of Caden kissing Jami's cheek] Happy couple!

I looked at Luke. "Quick, pose for a picture!" I hadn't told anyone Luke was home yet, so this was about to be a double surprise.

Me: [Picture of Luke and Edie smiling] This is the best thing we've ever heard!

Kristy: WHAT?!

Sam: Finally.

Jami: We promise not to steal the thunder at your wedding.

Jami: ...but maybe you should elope?

After responding with *talk to you later*, I turned off my phone and snuggled back into Luke. He kissed my forehead. "What do you think about eloping?"

I laughed and kissed him hard.

Edie's Tip #1: Never ever, ever, ever (again) give up on love.

The end.

LOVE EDIE'S AUTO SHOP AND GRENADINE?

Vera and Jack's wild ride is coming soon.

For sneak peeks, deleted scenes, and the latest book news, Make sure to subscribe to Heather's newsletter at www.HeatherNovak.net and follow Heather on Amazon at amazon.com/author/heathernovak!

ACKNOWLEDGMENTS

A huge, huge thank you to you readers! Time is our most precious commodity. Thank you for spending your time on my words.

The biggest thank you goes to Mr. Heather, my very own Prince Charming. Thanks for rolling with late nights, early mornings, dirty dishes, and rescheduled date nights. I literally wouldn't be able to do this without you. You're my favorite human.

Thank you to Lindee Robinson Photography and Najla Qamber Designs for my amazing cover, and to Danielle for all my logos. And of course, my human and canine models Michael Pack, Alexis Susalla, and Banner (and your families) for bringing the characters to life.

Thanks to Janna. You know what you did.

And Amber, for her Edie-isms.

Ellie at My Brother's Editor—you are awesome. Thanks for understanding that deadlines and I get along like cats and baths.

My assistant, Nicole, you are the reason anything gets done.

Michelle, you are an amazing alpha reader and I couldn't do this without you.

Thanks Erika (Myra) and Iveta for being wonderful proofreaders!

Big thanks to my sensitivity readers and translators Matt, Tamicka (T-Money), Andrea, Chie, Claire, and Kevin.

To Elyssa, who heard about this book for approximately 382,374,985 hours. Thank you for being alive.

For Tori, who taught me how to write sex positive, consensual romance and still educates me on life all the time. I want to be cool like you when I grow up.

A HUGE thank you to the Heather Novak Taco-tastic Fan Club —I really freaking love y'all! I don't know what I did to deserve you but you make me so happy.

To my author friends, my book nerds, the Greater Detroit Romance Writers chapter, the SOA—your support means the world.

Thanks to Lucie and her crew for keeping my office from eating me alive and for killing the spiders.

To Girls Auto Clinic for being an amazing resource! Check them out at girlsautoclinic.com.

I'm forever thankful for Kelli Ireland, Chris B., and Matt M. for your car knowledge! And of course, NPR's *Car Talk* needs a shout-out.

To my family! I love you. To all the friends I never see because I work all the time—I adore you. And finally, to my late mother, who gave me her love of books, writing, and social justice. As always, this book's for you.

ABOUT THE AUTHOR

Bold, Breathtaking, Badass Romance.

When she's not pretending to be a rock star with purple hair, Heather Novak is crafting sex positive romance novels to make you swoon! After her rare disease tried to kill her, Heather mutated into a superhero whose greatest power is writing romance that you can't put down.

When she's not obsessively reading or writing, Heather is trying to save the world like her late mama taught her.

Heather lives in the coolest city in the world, Detroit, Michigan, with Mr. Heather and their hypoallergenic pets.

Follow her at www.HeatherNovak.net

Made in the USA
Middletown, DE
21 November 2018